"How could a mother stay away from this beautiful baby?"

Martha put on a brave smile. "Yes. Well, let's try this bottle. I purely hope she'll drink from it." When she took Babykins from Abe, she discovered the baby had fallen asleep. "We better wait until she wakes up," she said. "You're a pretty good father," she added.

Abe barely knew what to think. "That may be what I am," he said, nodding. "I can't believe she really did it. Ran off and left her very own flesh and blood to the mercy of—whoever chooses to take her."

When the baby wakened, she knew exactly what to do to get milk from the bottle and did it with zest. But she fell asleep before she emptied it. Martha had filled it up, not knowing how much Babykins took each time.

Martha and Abe went to bed, still in shock. Were they to be the parents of that little baby forever? Abe couldn't fall asleep. "How about it, Lord?" he asked. "Is Nellie really gone? Is she coming back?"

You're doing fine, Abe.

VERALEE WIGGINS is the author of many novels, including *Llama Lady* and *Heartbreak Trail* which were voted top favorites by **Heartsong Presents** club members.

Books by VeraLee Wiggins

HEARTSONG PRESENTS

Don't miss out on any of our super romances. Write to us at the following address for information on our newest releases and club information.

Heartsong Presents Readers' Service
P.O. Box 719
Uhrichsville, OH 44683

A New
Love

VeraLee Wiggins

The Forerunners

Heartsong Presents

This is the final book of the "Forerunners Series." I find it fitting to dedicate it to its author, VeraLee Wiggins, who passed away on December 24, 1995 at the age of 67 years. She was my beloved wife and constant companion for over 50 years.

I wish to thank Stephen Reginald and all those at **Heartsong Presents** who made this series possible. God bless all of you.

Leroy Wiggins

ISBN 1-55748-911-4

A NEW LOVE

Cover illustration by Kathy Arbuckle.

PRINTED IN THE U.S.A.

one

Abram Noble and his wife Martha stood in the early April sunshine in their greening vegetable garden, hugging each other. "We'll be all right as long as we have God and each other," Martha assured him. "What else do we need?"

Abe grinned and pulled her close again. She referred to the horrifying winter they'd just endured. The temperature had plummeted to 29 degrees below zero in December, and hadn't risen to zero until a month ago, March 1862. They had lost almost all their livestock—two horses and nearly two hundred cattle, in which they'd invested their entire fortune.

Everyone in Walla Walla Valley, Washington Territory, had suffered like losses. The newspaper, *The Washington Statesman*, had said fewer than five hundred of the 35,000 head of livestock in the valley had survived the horrendous winter. Many people had lost their lives too.

Abe hugged Martha tightly. "You're right. God and each other are all we need. But it feels purty good to have something to eat once in a while." He released her and looked over their place, a 160-acre donation land claim. Last year it had produced abundantly, enough to almost make them rich. Then they'd spent the money on the cattle that had died.

"The garden won't produce for a couple of months," he said with a sigh. "I could make some more furniture to sell, but no one has any money left to buy it." He lifted her face and kissed her soundly.

A loud pretended vomit interrupted Martha and Abe. "You're making me sick," Willie said. "Can I go for a ride? Speck says he wants to."

Martha wiggled out of Abe's arms and hurried to Willie, her seven-year-old brother. "You're just jealous," she said, hugging him. "We purely love you too, but you won't let us hug you much." Martha and Willie's parents had died on the Oregon Trail, which they'd learned to call Heartbreak Trail.

Abe took Willie's hand and they walked together to the barn to saddle Willie's pony Speck, who'd somehow made it through the winter.

"Come on, Josie," Martha said to her gray, white, and black shepherd, hurrying toward the log house. "We'll start some bread and beans for supper."

She had the beans boiling on her bright-black wood cook stove, and half the flour in the bread when Abe came in and plopped into a chair beside the table. "I'm thankful Willie's horse made it," he said. "Willie may not have been able to understand what had happened." He raised his eyebrows. "For that matter I don't understand either."

Martha pummeled the bread, then began kneading it vigorously. "We don't. But we're better able to—"

The front door opened, interrupting her words. Three tall Indians marched in, straight as young trees, two dressed in white man's worn clothes and one in Indian buckskins. All wore moccasins.

Indians walked into any house in the valley, asking for food. Settlers always complied, rather than have a confrontation. The government had recently set aside reservations, but many Indians didn't believe that white men had the right to tell them where to live. These who had just walked in lived in a little community of tepees west of Walla Walla.

Others lived in tepees south of the Street, the Nez Percé, trail the town seemed to be building around.

"Food," the older man said.

"Gray Wolf!" Martha squealed. "Pony Boy! Camas! I'm so glad to see you." Then she pulled chairs out across the table from Abe. "Come sit down while I find something for you to eat."

Abe stood up. The fish oil the Indians smeared over themselves, thinking it would keep them warm, bothered Abe much more than it did Martha. "Sorry," Abe said, "I have to go out and see what I can do."

When Abe went out he left the door open. Pony Boy watched him leave. "Abe mad?"

Martha laughed and shook her dark head. "No, he's just afraid we're going to starve to death." She laughed again. "Not really. But he is worried. We have nothing left." She sliced the last loaf of bread and spread it with wild strawberry jam she'd made last summer. Putting the slices on small plates, she pushed them to the Indians, then asked the Lord to bless the food and the Indians. "Sorry I don't have any meat," she said. "No one does right now."

While the Indians ate, Martha finished kneading her bread and put it to rise. "Shall we work on our languages awhile?" she asked when each finished his second slice. For two years Martha had been teaching these Indians her language and learning theirs. They understood each other well now, using bits of both English and Nez Percé.

Gray Wolf, the other two Indians' father, shook his head. "We talk gold."

"Yes." Martha remembered. The Indians had told her and Abe that they knew where there was lots of easy-to-get gold, and had offered to take them there. "We don't know whether our God wants us to go after it," she said. "We have to wait until He tells us."

"How God talk?" Camas asked.

Martha thought a moment. "He talks to Abe," she said. "He and Abe carry on conversations. With me, He talks to my heart and helps me to understand what He wants."

"When God say?" Pony Boy wanted to know.

Martha shook her head. "I don't know. We're waiting."

Gray Wolf moved close to Martha. He pointed at the ceiling, then patted his chest. "Martha God talk Gray Wolf. Now."

If he'd sounded that determined the first time they met, Martha would have been terrified, but now she knew these Nez Percé men were kind and friendly.

She shook her head. "He talks when He wants to talk, Gray Wolf. We don't tell Him to do things."

"No talk Gray Wolf?"

Martha put her hand on his arm. "He does, Gray Wolf. He talks to everyone in the world but sometimes people don't listen. Most people don't listen." She cupped her hand behind her ear. "You listen. Maybe you'll hear Him."

The graying Indian shook his head. "No like Indians."

"Yes, He does, Gray Wolf. He loves everyone. He loves you as much as He loves me."

Soon the Indians filed through the open door. "Martha God say go, get much gold." As they marched proudly across the prairie, Martha opened the other door and all the windows. She always tried to get rid of the smell before Abe came in.

Martha cleaned the house and had the beans and bread ready when Abe came back with Willie following him.

As they eagerly ate the beans and bread, Martha reminded Abe of the Indians' offer to get them some gold. "We purely need it bad," she said.

Abe shoved half a thick heel of warm bread into his mouth. "We do," he said. "It would help us get on our feet again." After eating silently for a few more minutes he raised his eyes to Martha. "Thing is we don't want that gold unless God wants us to have it. He may have a better plan." An impish grin spread across his face. "Haven't you heard hard times draw us closer to God? That's really what we want, Martha. To be close to God."

"Of course we do," Martha replied. "But we are close to Him, Abe. And I want what He wants just as much as you do. But we don't know what He wants yet. Maybe you could talk to Him tonight."

Abe nodded. "I'll try to do that if I don't fall asleep first. Or if He don't."

Willie burst out laughing. "Abe! God doesn't sleep."

As Martha prepared to serve a rice pudding, someone pounded on the front door.

Abe grinned. "We know it isn't the Indians." He opened the door to Martha's aunt and uncle who lived across the creek.

"We got lonely so here we are," Aunt Mandy said. She pulled Willie to her. "How's my boy tonight?"

Martha served everyone rice pudding. "I want cream on mine," Willie said.

Abe chuckled. "You know we don't have that stuff anymore, Willie. If it'd help, we'd all fuss for some."

"How are Riley and Melissa?" Martha asked. The two were Mandy and Cleave's son and his wife, both dear to Martha and Abe.

"They're fine," Uncle Cleave said. "Got through the cold better'n most. Mostly 'cause they didn't have any cattle to worry with. What about Jackson and Nellie?"

"They made it too," Abe said. "Those two seem to live on love no matter what the weather." Jackson and Nellie were Martha's brother and wife. Abe referred to Jackson's obvious preference to enjoying his wife rather than work.

"How does Luke like the new work horse you bought?" Uncle Cleave wanted to know. The unprecedented winter had killed John, one of Abe's prized Belgian team. He'd bought another work horse with money they'd found in Martha's covered wagon—money that had belonged to her parents. "You getting your place worked up with them?"

"Work together almost as well as Luke and John did," Abe said. "Got the place all plowed and most of it disked. We're about ready to plant. How about you?"

"Doin' fine. The new oxen're young but catchin' on. Riley's eager to use 'em. Soon's some more animals come in he's plannin' to buy his own." Uncle Cleave pushed back his chair. "Seen the last paper?" he asked. "Says thousands of miners're waitin' in the Dalles fer the river to get low enough for the steamboats to navigate. That'll be right soon now. Says they'll be hoofin' it to Walla Walla where they 'spect to find animals, food, and gear fer minin'. Wonder what we're gonna feed 'em."

Abe shook his head. "This'd be a real bonanza if we hadn't all been froze out. Well, we'll just do the best we can." He thought a moment and a frown crossed his face. "Crime's been gettin' pretty awful. No tellin' what it'll be like as more people crowd in. Town may not be fit to live in."

The next morning Abe awakened looking radiant. "What happened to you?" Martha asked. "You look like a plate of fried sunshine."

"I feel like one too," Abe answered. "We're plantin' hay

this year so we can go after some gold! We'll leave as soon as it's in the ground."

A thrill ripped through Martha that brought out a gasp. "He told you it's all right! Didn't He Abe?"

"Yep. And to get the hay in the ground quick. He knew we needed the gold real bad."

"How long will it take to plant the hay?"

Abe thought a moment. "Three weeks if we work from dawn to dusk. Think the Indians'll be back by then?"

She nodded. The Indians were eager to get going. "Long before that, Abe. Do you think they'll let Jackson and Nellie, and Riley and Melissa go too?"

They hurried to the fields and didn't come home until after dark. As Martha warmed up beans and split peas for supper, a thought crossed her mind. "How are we going, Abe? We don't have horses."

"We'll take the wagon and work horses. That way we can carry plenty of beans and side meat."

Three days later the Indians returned. When Martha saw them, she ran in from the field. "Food," Gray Wolf said.

Martha smiled. No matter how good of friends they became she still always had to feed them. She gave them bread and strawberry jam again.

"Martha man talk God?" Gray Wolf asked while they ate.

"Yes!" Martha said with joy. "We're going after the gold, Gray Wolf. But we have to finish planting the hay first."

"When?"

"About three weeks. Can we take some of our family with us, Gray Wolf?"

He swung his head back and forth. "Abe, Martha, Indians. Martha, Abe, Indians."

Martha felt strong disappointment. She'd have felt much

safer with a larger group. A larger group of her own people. But maybe the Indians felt safer when they had a majority.

The Indians returned one evening about a week before they planned to leave. "Have horses?" Pony Boy asked.

Abe grinned and pointed toward the barn. "Out there, Pony Boy. We'll take the big horses and the wagon."

Gray Wolf nearly jumped into the air. "No wagon! Too much loud."

Abe looked surprise. "We need a wagon, Gray Wolf, to haul our supplies. Besides we don't have saddle horses. Ours are all dead."

Gray Wolf settled back down. "No wagon," he repeated softly. "Ride Indians' horses."

"What about food?" Martha asked.

"Indians get food," Camas said. "Good food."

Martha looked at Abe. He smiled. "I think if we want to go on this expedition, we do it their way. All right, Gray Wolf. We'll ride your horses and eat your food."

Gray Wolf nodded. "Good." He grinned at Martha. "Long time eat Martha food."

"Yes," Martha said, "but I didn't mind. We've gained some good friends." Then Martha remembered Josie. "Can I bring my dog?" she asked.

Pony Boy grinned broadly, then the grin left. "No eat dog," he said.

"Dog much loud," Camas said. "No eat dog."

Martha wondered what they meant. Then she remembered the first time they'd asked for food. She'd lived in her wagon then. All she'd had was flour and water. When she'd cooked that for them they'd become angry and offered to eat her dog. She raised her eyes to Pony Boy's. "No, I'd never eat my dog. Josie's my good friend. I'll leave her home."

Martha asked Aunt Mandy if she'd keep Willie and Josie while they went with the Indians. She didn't say any more and her aunt didn't ask.

The first day on the road Martha felt strange. After all, what did she know about these three Indians? Only that they came for food and English lessons. She also knew they felt extremely grateful for Abe's saving Pony Boy's life when he'd been accused of a murder he didn't commit. That's why the Indians offered to help them.

Noon came and the Indians let the horses drink but didn't stop for a meal for the people.

As it grew dark that evening, the Indians led them to a protected place to spend the night, and staked the horses to graze. The Indians left for a little while and returned with several kinds of leaves and roots. Also five fish. Martha noticed the Indians didn't disturb a leaf, stick, or stone while they walked. She didn't even hear them return until they appeared in the clearing.

Camas made a fire while Pony Boy cleaned the fish and Gray Wolf fixed the roots and leaves. "Why can't I help?" Martha asked.

"Indians cook," Gray Wolf said.

A short time later the Indians offered Abe and Martha a fine banquet, everything served on the stick they'd cooked it on. Abe asked to thank His God for the food and the Indians agreed. Martha ate all she could hold and noticed Abe ate even more. As Martha wondered what she would do with a delicious root, a squirrel ventured near. She held out her hand to the shy little animal. It backed away. Then it crept nearer. Finally it reached Martha's hand. Snatching the food, it turned and raced off through the forest.

Only a few moments later a large bird swooped down from

a tree, caught the screaming squirrel in its talons and flew back to the same bough.

Everyone watched in shocked silence. Finally Camas spoke. "Sign. Bad luck." He shook his head.

"Not good," Gray Wolf agreed.

"Wait a minute," Abe said. "We don't have to depend on luck. Our God takes care of us." He asked Martha to pray with him and they both thanked God for being with them through the day and asked His protection during the night.

When they finished, Martha opened her eyes to find all the Indians staring at them.

"White man God live in sky?" Camas asked.

"Yes," Abe said. Then he patted his chest. "Our God lives right here too, in Abe's heart where He hears our prayers."

Gray Wolf nodded.

"Luck good," Pony Boy said.

"Abe God make luck good," Camas said. "Good God."

The next day they met several groups of white men heading for Walla Walla. "Any luck in the mines?" Abe asked several times.

two

But no one wanted to talk about gold. Everyone seemed to be looking over his shoulder, fearful of who might be following. Abe thought he understood. If a person could get away with anything in Walla Walla, who would protect a man from thieves on this long lonely trail?

Every night they camped beside some sort of stream and every night the Indians somehow found a fish for everyone. For breakfast they each had another fish and more roots. They didn't eat anything between.

When the Sabbath Day came, Abe wondered if they'd be able to stop and rest. He should have settled that important point before they started. "Forgive me, Father," he said softly, "for overlooking Your special day when we planned this trip. Soften their hearts and help us teach them about You."

Start planning your lesson, Abe.

Abe grinned. "Thanks, Lord. I knew You would help us."

When Abe asked the Indians if they could stop and worship the Great Spirit, they agreed so quickly that Abe could only silently thank God again for preparing the way.

Abe told them how much God loves them. "Do you know how far away the stars are?" he asked them.

"Long way," Camas replied.

"Far," Pony Boy agreed.

Abe showed them his Bible as he had many times before. "My God's book says He loves us as much as the stars are high. And as deep as the sea. He loves us much. He loves every one of us that much and it makes Him feel bad when

15

we hurt each other."

The Indians seemed happy to listen to Abe talk about his God.

One evening after they'd been traveling eight days they came to what the Indians called "Big Water."

"I think this is the Snake River," Martha told Abe. "Remember I told you about the little boy, Pete, who drowned in the Snake? It looked like this."

They followed the river and that evening Abe and Martha went with the Indians to get some fish. The Indians didn't use poles, but just put worms or flies on hooks attached to some kind of cord and dropped it into the water. Soon they started pulling fish from the water, some too big for one person to eat.

"We're having a feast tonight," Abe said. "We won't need anything else."

After awhile Abe and Martha walked on down the river a ways watching the ducks and geese. Suddenly Abe saw something swimming lazily a few feet beneath the surface. He'd never seen a creature like it. He leaned over the water, pointing. "Look, Martha, I see an alligator! There, swimming under the water."

Martha searched through the murky water for a minute. "Yes! I see it, Abe. Isn't it the strangest looking thing you've ever seen?" She watched it another moment. "But it isn't an alligator, Abe. Alligators have legs. I think it's a sturgeon! That's a prehistoric fish with scales like an alligator. I read about them in a book. How long is it?"

Abe peered into the water. "Looks to be about ten feet to me." He raised his eyes to hers. "All right, how long is a sturgeon?"

"The book said they grow to fourteen feet and weigh three thousand pounds in the Great Lakes. I don't know if they grow bigger or smaller here."

"Well, they aren't much smaller."

Martha put her arm around his waist. "Know what else it said about the big ones? By the time they get really big they're two or three hundred years old. That's purely older than we are, Abe."

After watching the sturgeon awhile, they went back to the Indians and told them about the great fish. The Indians wanted to see it, but it was gone.

After they followed the Snake River another day, the Indians showed them a place where the river flowed shallow and wide. "We cross," Gray Wolf said pointing across the river.

Martha's face turned white and her hands clenched her horse's reins. Abe knew she remembered the horrible crossing where the little boy drowned. He rode as close to her as his horse would go. "It's nothing," he said softly. "The horses won't even have to swim."

Pony Boy overheard and nodded. "Horses swim."

Oh. Abe tried again. "Well, it won't be bad. Nothing like where you crossed in the wagons." He turned to Gray Wolf. "Could you go first? Martha's pretty nervous. She saw a little boy drown in this river."

Gray Wolf nodded and motioned for his two sons to follow him. Abe moved a little closer to Martha and leaned across the two horses for her hand. The Indians rode single file and almost reached the other side before the water deepened enough to force the horses into a swim. With hardly any current, the horses didn't even struggle but hit the bank straight across.

"Ready?" Abe asked Martha. Silently, he asked God to be with her and strengthen her.

She urged her horse into the stream, lips straight and tense, her back like a piece of wood. As the horse moved across, Martha seemed to relax some. Abe rode behind. "I'm right here," he called. "You're doin' great but I'm watching every move just in case." Martha reached the deep place and her horse started swimming. Abe felt the cold for her as her horse dropped deeper into the water until it came to Martha's waist. She said nothing.

Then they stood in the sun on the east side of the river. Martha slid off her horse laughing happily. "Abe, I told you it wasn't anything." She laughed again at her absurdity.

They followed the Clearwater River and the next day Abe showed Martha and the Indians where the Spalding Mission stood a ways off the trail. "The Spaldings and the Whitmans came from far away to teach you Indians about our Great God," he said.

Gray Wolf grunted. "Poison Indians. Give Indians food. Make sick. Give medicine sick papooses. Papooses die."

Martha and Abe looked at each other in shock. "I've never heard that," Abe said after recovering somewhat. The horses plodded on.

"Hear Indians kill missionary?" Pony Boy asked.

Martha glanced at Abe. "He means the horrible massacre in '47."

"Yes, we heard," Abe said. "Do you know anything about that?"

Gray Wolf nodded. "White papooses sick. Red spots. Indians get spots too. White doctor give medicine. White papooses get well. Indians die."

"I don't know, Gray Wolf," Abe said. "I've never heard that at all."

Gray Wolf's back straightened even more than usual. "True. Know watermelons?"

Abe grinned. "We sure do," he said. "We been raising a lot to sell. Muskmelons too."

Gray Wolf nodded. "Doctor put medicine in watermelons make Indians sick. Bad sick."

Abe could hardly take this in. "You mean he gave Indians watermelons with poison?" He met Martha's eyes. "Why would he do that?" The horses had taken advantage of the intense conversation by slowing almost to a stop.

Martha shook her head no.

Gray Wolf gave a little hoot and nudged his horse with his heels. His horse picked up its speed and the others followed. Then he grinned at Abe. "Indians take watermelons. Doctor not like."

Oh. Now Abe saw. The Indians had been stealing Whitman's watermelons and the missionary put something in them to make the thieves sorry. Anyway, if this far fetched story was accurate that was probably what happened. "I see," he told Gray Wolf, "but that doesn't explain why he'd poison Indian babies who were sick."

Gray Wolf shook his head. "Not like Indians. Not want papooses grow up."

Three days later the Indians led Martha and Abe off the trail through dense trees and brush.

"How do you know where you're going?" Martha asked when they camped beside a small stream that night.

"How long does this go on?" Abe added.

"To gold," Camas said.

"Two, three days," Pony Boy said.

The next day they wound through the thick woods, around small and larger hills, until Abe had no idea where they were. He chuckled to himself. Probably exactly what the Indians had in mind. As they meandered east and south, all the trees looked alike to Abe and so did the hills covered with more trees.

Two days later the Indians spread out single file and rode close to one of the larger hills. In the afternoon they stopped and unsaddled the horses, then tethered them so they could graze. "Walk," Camas said. "Horses make loud."

Abe took Martha's hand and they followed the three Indians, who seemed to make no sound at all as they neared a steep hill. As he listened to the silence ahead, he thought he and Martha must have stepped on every brittle stick in the woods. "Why do we have to be quiet, anyhow?" he asked. "We're the only living beings in these hills."

Gray Wolf dropped back beside them. "Much living things," he whispered. "Indian Reservation. Nez Percé. Indians living. Bears living too."

Abe pulled Martha closer to him. "You better stay close to me," he murmured. "I might be able to save you from an Indian." He chuckled. "Of course, I'll run from a bear. But I'll drag you along if I can."

The Indians led them ever closer to the steep hill. Finally they disappeared behind some tall bushes. It seemed the bushes grew right against the hill but Abe kept walking. When he reached the spot where he'd last seen the Indians, he found the trees tight against the hill just as he'd thought. But as he forced his way under the trees, he found a small opening in the mountain. "So—they went in here," he said. Putting his arm around Martha, he stood with her in the opening and looked in. "It gets dark pretty fast," he said. "Wonder how they can see in there."

"I don't know," Martha said, "but I don't think they wanted us to follow."

Abe grinned. "I'll bet they hoped we wouldn't even find the opening. That's how come they hurried on ahead." Taking Martha's arm he led her away from the cave, out from the thick trees to an opening. Sun shone brightly where the trees weren't so close together. "We may as well sit down and rest. No telling how long they'll be in there."

"I hope they find something," Martha said. "The trip's been fun, but it'll be more fun if we have some gold to help the others and buy things we need when we get home."

Abe lay on the fresh green grass beside her in the warm sunshine, leaning up on his left arm. He traced over her nose, over her mouth, and around her chin with his right index finger. "Did I ever tell you how completely beautiful you are?" he asked quietly. "And how much I love you? This trip will still be perfect if we don't find a penny's worth of gold. Think of all the time we got to spend together. Not working. Not running somewhere doing something. Just riding along together." He leaned over her and kissed her gently, sweetly. "And this," he finished.

"You're making me blush, Abram Noble. You're really noble." She giggled. "I mean it, Abe. You're truly good. Which reminds me. I've been wanting to tell you how sorry I am for waiting so long to be a real wife to you. I know now how unfair it was for you."

Their love had been so special that Abe hadn't thought of their unreal marriage for a long time. "It was kinda hard," he admitted. Then he remembered God's part in it. Martha had lived in a covered wagon. Her food had run out, she didn't have any money and the snow was starting to fly. "But hey! It was all God's idea. He told me to do it. He not only told me to do it, He insisted. And kept on insisting until I asked you. He told me I would be blessed more than I could imagine. He knew how it would all end up." Abe couldn't help it. He gathered her close and held her tightly for a long time.

They both fell asleep. When Abe opened his eyes the stars twinkled overhead. No moon appeared to send silver beams into their quiet world. He shook Martha gently. "Are you ready to wake up?" he whispered.

She jerked and sat up, looking around. "Aren't they back yet?" she whispered. "Haven't you seen them at all?"

Abe grinned in the dark and shook his head. "Not a glimpse. You know what that means don't you? They're getting lots and lots of gold for us."

Martha giggled. "Or they can't find any—and now they can't find their way out. I'm hungry, Abe. How about you?"

"My stomach's been rumblin' for hours." After a quiet moment he laughed. "You got somethin' to eat tucked in a pocket somewhere?" He felt her shaking her head.

They talked quietly for another hour, waiting for their three friends to appear. "What if they don't come back?" Martha finally asked.

Abe thought that over. "Well, I reckon we'll take the horses and go home. I'm not sure we'll be able to find food but we'll get home somehow."

Abe began to pray softly, "Dear Father in heaven, we thank You for being so close to us. And for loving us so much You gave Your only Son to die for our sins so we can live forever with You. We thank You for blessing our trip so far and we pray You'll keep right on blessing it real good. Be with the Indians, God, and bring them safely out of that dark hole in the mountain. Thank You, Father, in Jesus' name."

Pretty soon Martha fell asleep again. As she slept, Abe gently rubbed her back and arms. "Thank You, God, for giving me this best woman in the world."

There's none better, Abe. You take good care of her.

"I will, Father. Thanks." He crowded close to Martha and fell asleep.

☙

"Abe, wake up." Abe stirred at Martha's voice. He discovered the sun shining brightly and Martha bending over him.

He jumped up beside her. "Are they back?"

She shook her head. "No. Do you think we should do something?"

"Yeah. We better find something to eat. My stomach's stickin' to my back right now."

They searched around, finding several weeds they knew were edible. After about an hour of hunting food Abe grinned at Martha. "Now I know why cows eat all day long."

"Why?"

"Because it takes them that long to get filled up." They laughed together as they continued finding and eating weeds. "Maybe we should be eating the roots," Abe said. They stacked up a pile of weeds for the Indians as they picked and ate.

A little before noon something touched Abe's arm as he pulled an extra tough weed. He jerked around to find Camas. Pony Boy and Gray Wolf followed several feet behind. All three carried burlap bags that looked heavy. Abe laughed out loud. "Where'd you get the bags?" he asked Camas.

"White man. Wapotatoes. Ready go?"

"Yeah. We're ready. What'd you find? How come it took so long?"

Gray Wolf set his bag on the ground. "Plenty gold. Got lost."

Abe couldn't help laughing. "Martha," he said, "our guides got lost. Do you believe that?"

"Gold long way," Gray Wolf said. "Dark. Find gold. Much tunnels. Lost." He opened his bag and motioned Abe to look inside. When Abe complied, he couldn't believe what he saw. Lots of large chunks. Maybe ten pounds altogether. But it didn't look very gold.

He raised his eyes to Gray Wolf's. "You sure this is gold?"

Gray Wolf smiled and nodded. "Gold. Look other sacks."

Abe took Martha's hand and led her to the other two bags. They looked the same but held more gold then Gray Wolf's.

"How much of this is ours?" Martha asked Abe softly.

Before he could tell her he didn't know, Pony Boy answered. "Gold Abe's," he said. "Save Pony Boy hang."

Abe shook his head. "You don't owe me anything, Pony Boy. I just happened along at the right time." He wondered how much the gold was worth and decided to ask.

"Not know," Gray Wolf answered. "Much money." He met Abe's gaze. "More in cave."

Abe smiled to himself. The Indians were generous to give Martha and him some of their gold but their secret remained a secret. He had no idea how to get it. When they reached the trail again he wouldn't even be able to find the cave. Anyway, he had a strong feeling the Indians had stashed that gold in the cave, that it had come from somewhere else.

After the Indians ate the pile of weeds, Camas led the way to the horses where they put the gold in the saddle bags, saddled the horses, and secured the bags behind the saddles so they didn't appear very full. They took off the way they'd come, with only a few weeds in their stomachs since yesterday morning. But Abe felt great anyway. There was more to a man than food in his stomach.

"Thank You, God," he whispered as they followed the Indians through the trees and brush. He still felt completely lost.

They stopped early that evening and enjoyed the bounty the Indians provided. Two fish each and several kinds of roots baked in the fire.

Two days later they reached the trail and Abe heaved a sigh. Now he could find his way home. Not that he'd need to with the Indians guiding them.

The Indians seemed happy and contented as they rode homeward. They stopped again for the Sabbath Day. Abe and Martha taught the Indians several songs during their little service. Abe could hardly keep a straight face as they tried to sing the hymns in their broken English.

He asked Martha to talk to them.

"We already told you God made the people and the world," she said. "He loved them because He made them, and He came and walked with them each day in the beautiful garden home He made for them. He gave them many kinds of luscious fruit to eat from the trees. He told them they could eat all they wanted from any tree in the garden except one. He said they couldn't eat from that tree because it wasn't good for them and they'd die if they ate that fruit.

"Adam and Eve loved their garden home and didn't think anything of that tree until the devil disguised himself as a snake and talked to Eve. He told her the fruit of that tree was good to eat and they wouldn't die if they ate it. And that they'd become like God if they did. So Eve tried it and found it tasted good. She gave Adam some of it too, and they began to grow old right then. People have died ever since.

"But God loved His people and didn't want them to die. He made a plan to stop people from dying. I'll tell you about that next Sabbath if we're still on the trail." She giggled. "I'll tell you about it anyway if you'd like to hear."

"Indians hear," Pony Boy said.

They started on the trail early the next morning, their stomachs full of the good things the Indians had found for them. A few hours later they neared the Spalding Mission again. Abe wondered if they'd get into a discussion about the missionaries again.

As he thought about what he'd tell the Indians, two riders approached from behind, riding hard. "Stop!" one of them yelled. "Stop right there or we'll shoot you dead!"

"Come!" Gray Wolf said, kicking his horse hard. "Hurry!"

"Hurry, Martha," Abe said. "They don't mean us any good."

In less than a minute the four horses stretched their legs in long galloping strides. "Maybe we can get to the Spalding Mission," Martha puffed.

three

Martha thought she'd never felt such fear in her life. "Help us, Father!" she called loudly. The men yelled, the horses hooves beat the ground, but she knew God heard anyway. "Thank You, Lord," she added.

As they cut the distance between them and the mission, she began to think they might get away. The men fired several shots but didn't hit anyone. Finally Martha saw the mission and heaved a big sigh of relief. When the men noticed that, they'd leave. She hoped.

But suddenly two more men appeared in the trail ahead of them, masked and mounted on big horses. Martha glanced at Gray Wolf, wondering where they could go. Surely he'd cut off through the woods.

"Stop them nags right now or we'll shoot 'em out from under you!" someone yelled. Gray Wolf pulled his horse to a stop and everyone followed his lead.

One of the other men moved his horse beside Martha while looking at Abe. "We know you got gold so git it. Now!"

Abe looked at Gray Wolf, who nodded almost imperceptibly. Abe slid off his horse, unfastened his saddle bag, pulled out the burlap bag of gold and handed it to one of the men. "How'd you know we had gold?" he asked almost civilly.

"We watch everyone goin' through. Ain't hard to tell." He turned to Gray Wolf, aiming his rifle at the Indian's head. "Get off that horse, redskin, and get the rest." Martha glanced around and found guns pointed at them from every direction.

Gray Wolf dismounted, pulled out his burlap bag and handed

it to the man. "Take part, leave part," he said sullenly.

The man laughed nastily. "Why would I do that, you savage? Now get the rest."

Gray Wolf looked directly where the man's eyes slitted through the mask. "Gray Wolf no have more."

The man cracked Gray Wolf over the head with the butt of his gun. "Get it, redskin. Before I lose my patience!"

Gray Wolf marched over to Martha's horse and looked into her saddle bag, then shook his head. "No."

A shot rang out and Martha thought Gray Wolf had been hit. But he didn't fall. She looked at the other men to find one of them lowering his rifle. He'd shot into the air.

"The next one's for you, Injun!" the man called out.

Gray Wolf ambled to Pony Boy and took his saddle bag. He pulled out the last bag of gold and threw it at the man. Then he turned and mounted his horse. "Go," he said and started down the path. His two sons followed, then Abe and Martha fell in behind. Martha expected to hear shots but only an eerie silence shrouded the area.

A few moments later the four thieves passed them at full gallup.

"Well," Abe said dropping back beside her. "I guess we all get to live. That's somethin'." He turned his face upward. "Thanks, God. Money would have been nice but life and health are necessary." He grinned at Martha. "And someone to love."

The Indians didn't say a word for hours. Neither did they hurry their horses. They said a few words in their own language, but Martha couldn't hear well enough to understand.

That night they stopped early. Martha and Abe waited at the campsite for their friends. "I'd like to help," Abe said, "but they seem to want to be alone while they fish and hunt roots."

Martha had been wanting to talk to Abe. They sat on a downed tree trunk. "Well, what do you think, Abe? Are you terribly disappointed?"

He looked thoughtful, then shook his head and grinned. "We aren't any worse off than when we started. We've had a nice trip and learned to know the Indians better. All we have to do now is figure out how we're goin' to live until our crops give us some money."

Martha smiled at him. "What you're trying to say is you are purely disappointed but won't let it get you down."

Abe hugged her close. "I guess that's about it." He pointed his thumb upward. "With Him up there takin' care of us we'll be just fine. It won't hurt us to depend on Him for our food."

The Indians soon came back with fish, roots, and some kind of berries. After the good meal Camas told Abe and Martha to come. They followed through some brush to a clearing where a beautiful little blue lake sparkled before them. "Fish here," Pony Boy said.

They sat on some rocks on the shore and enjoyed the lake for a couple of hours, talking quietly. Martha wished Abe would talk to them about the gold, but he didn't. The Indians didn't say anything either. When the sun turned the sky to gold and orange, they went back to camp. Abe had started having a little worship service each night and the Indians seemed to enjoy it.

This night he asked Martha to talk to them so she continued the story she'd started last Sabbath. "Remember how Adam and Eve ate the bad tree? Well, God felt really bad about that because He loved Adam and Eve and He didn't want them to die. God couldn't tell them it was all right this one time because no one would believe Him anymore. So many years later He sent His only Son to die for men, to take the punishment man deserved, so they could live again. He did that, Gray Wolf, so you and I can live forever with Him. He did it for you, too, Pony Boy and Camas." She turned to Abe. "He did it for you too, Abe. He loves you even more than I do. I don't see how there could be more love than I have for you, but He loves you more.

"All we have to do is to accept the big sacrifice He made for us and love Him with all our hearts and our minds and our strength and our soul. That's all."

The Indians said nothing but looked very thoughtful. When Abe asked them to bow for prayer they all did.

"Gray Wolf talk God," Gray Wolf said. Then he began: "Gray Wolf want love God. Want live God. God, come love Gray Wolf."

Abe moved quickly to Gray Wolf's side. "You're now a child of God," he said. "God loves you and will take you to live with Him forever." He grinned at Gray Wolf. "Think you can put up with us forever? That's a long time."

Gray Wolf nodded. "Abe, Gray Wolf brother."

ↄ

Martha rejoiced over Gray Wolf as she and Abe lay side by side in the dark night. "Are you awake?" she whispered to him.

"I am now," he answered, pulling her close. "Somethin' wrong?"

"No. Now I know why we came. We're to make Christians of these wonderful men." She waited for Abe to answer but she heard only a quiet little snore. "Well, teaching them to love God's more important than gold," she told him even while he slept.

The next morning after they ate, Gray Wolf seemed agitated. "Is anything wrong?" Abe asked.

"Abe go gold?" Gray Wolf asked.

Abe looked at Martha. She shook her head. If they got more those men would probably take it away again. Why not go home and figure a way to get food.

"I guess we'd just like to go on home," Abe said grinning. "If we don't have something, they can't take it away."

The Indians didn't hurry at all that day. In fact Martha would have said they dawdled. She couldn't figure why and she couldn't ask Abe. The Indians understood too much English now for them to say anything they didn't want to share.

Two nights later Abe asked Martha to talk to them again. She'd been hoping he would, as she had something she wanted to say bad.

"You all know now that our big God will let you live with Him forever. But I want to tell you He's with you all the time right here." She put her hand over her heart. "If we love Him as much as we know how to love He'll live in our heart and help us and guide us."

The three Indians put their right hands over their hearts.

"God here. God help," Pony Boy said. "Love God. Help us."

Martha noticed Abe put his hand over his heart too.

"God talk Pony Boy?" the young Indian asked.

Martha nodded. "God does talk to us. But He doesn't talk to everyone the same way. He talks to Abe like a friend. He talks to me by feelings. You listen, Pony Boy, and He'll talk to you somehow."

"Gray Wolf wonder," the big Indian said, "big God not help. Men take gold."

Oh. "He kept the men from hurting us," she said. "We'll get along somehow without the gold. Maybe we'll be better off this way. Maybe He didn't really send us to get the gold,

Gray Wolf. I think He loved you men so much He sent us so we could teach you about Him."

Gray Wolf didn't say anymore but went off to bed with a serious look on his face.

The next morning the Indians were gone when Abe and Martha woke up. They soon appeared with fish, roots, and berries. After they ate they dawdled around camp awhile. Martha couldn't understand why they were so relaxed, as they'd hurried off every morning before.

When they finally started, the Indians actually let the horses graze along the way. Martha wished she could get a chance to see what Abe thought about it.

Two mornings later when she woke up to find the Indians gone, she let Abe sleep a little longer. The three hadn't returned by the time he finally got up. They still hadn't returned an hour later. "Must be having trouble finding fish or roots," Abe said. "I wish they'd let me fish. They could teach me a lot. I wouldn't mind knowing how to find food in the forest too." He grinned at her. "When we get lost, we'll just have to find weeds and eat all day."

They decided to do that now, so they found all the weeds they recognized and piled them beside the coals from last night's fire. "They may not even eat this stuff," Martha said. "But at least we tried."

Two hours later, about mid-morning, the Indians returned with not a sound. "What's this?" Abe asked.

The Indians rode three strange horses and led a fourth. A moment later they pulled the saddle bags from the horses. "Look," Camas said. Then he pulled out of his saddle bag a burlap bag that looked familiar. Camas opened it to reveal a bunch of gold. The others each had a bag too.

"What happened?" Abe asked. "How did you get these?"

Gray Wolf looked pleased. "Find bad men. Drink fire

water. Sleep."

Camas couldn't wait for Gray Wolf to finish. He cut right in. "Take horses. Guns. Gold. No take saddles. Bad men carry saddles."

"Horses call," Pony Boy continued. "Men sleep. Men wake up. Walk."

Abe burst into loud laughter. "You really got them. But what will they really do when they wake up?"

"Walk," Gray Wolf said with a rare smile. "Walk and walk and walk."

The Indians didn't want to take time to cook breakfast, so they all grabbed handfuls of the weeds Martha and Abe had gathered.

The Indians didn't let the horses dally anymore. They traveled late and got up early. And hurried the horses all day.

One evening they saw a flock of grouse. "Get guns," Camas said. "Eat birds."

"No, let's not," Martha said. "Let's just look at them. Aren't they pretty? They're a family, Camas, like we are."

They ate fish that night but the next night the Indians took their guns when they left. After awhile they heard a report. Martha shuddered, wondering what poor animal just lost its life.

Soon the Indians appeared with a dressed bird, much larger than a grouse. They started a fire, put a long limb through the bird, and barbecued it. Though somewhat tough, it didn't taste too bad. Wild, but definitely edible.

"What color was this bird?" Abe asked.

"Black," Camas said. "Red on head."

Martha felt her meal trying to come back up. Camas had just described a vulture, birds which ate only old rotten meat. After a few minutes she felt better and realized the Indians had shot the vulture because she didn't want them shooting pretty birds.

Several days later, they reached Walla Walla. Martha had never felt so happy to be home in her life. Home and safe! And with gold. *Thank You, God,* she said silently. The Indians would go west, out by Fort Walla Walla; Martha and Abe would go east to their farm.

The Indians reined in their horses. "Abe," Pony Boy said. Abe stopped his horse too. "Take horses," Pony Boy said, pointing to the thieves' horses. "Abe's horses."

Abe shook his head. "No, Pony Boy, I can't take them. They're yours. You earned them. I'll take Martha home, then bring back the horses we rode." He held a hand out to Pony Boy. "How do we ever thank you for the gold? It'll help us and our families get a new start." After shaking hands with Pony Boy, Abe repeated the action with Gray Wolf and Camas.

"Brother," Gray Wolf said when Abe shook hands with him. "Big God make brothers."

"Right," Abe said. "And don't you forget it. You come eat our food anytime." He laughed. "As soon as we get some. It won't take long, so you come, hear?"

Pony Boy drew near. "Indians go Abe's tepee. Take horses." Gray Wolf liked the idea, and they rode with them so Abe wouldn't have to return the horses and walk.

Martha couldn't wait to see Willie. She'd been his mother for a long time, and she'd worried a little about him while they were gone.

They stopped the horses by the door, took the saddle bags with the burlap bags inside, and hid them in their bedroom.

The front door slammed hard, and Willie grabbed Martha around the waist. "I thought something happened, Martha. Why were you gone so long?"

Martha sat on the bed and pulled her seven-year-old brother onto her lap. "We went a long way, Willie. We hurried." She leaned to his ear. "We got some gold too." She resumed her normal voice. "Now we can buy food. And one of these days we'll buy horses. Then I'll be able to ride with you and Speck."

"Tomorrow? Can you buy a horse tomorrow so I can ride a long ways?"

Uncle Cleave and Aunt Mandy came in then. "You look like you're all in one piece!" Uncle Cleave said in his usual stentorian voice. He and Mandy both hugged Martha and Willie in her lap.

Abe came out of the other bedroom. "We're fine. And had a great trip. Those Indians are faithful friends." He hugged Aunt Mandy and Willie and shook Uncle Cleave's hand. "Got a little gold too," he said. "I guess we'll have to find out what it's worth before we share it."

"We don't need any," Aunt Mandy said. "We didn't have all our money in livestock like you did. We still got plenty."

Aunt Mandy invited Abe and Martha for supper, an invitation Martha appreciated as she didn't have much in the house to eat.

The next morning after a breakfast of oatmeal, Abe turned to Martha. "How about going to the traders with me this morning? We can take a couple of pieces of gold and see what they think about it."

Martha hurried to put the dishes away, combed Willie's hair, and headed toward the Street with Abe, bubbling over with excitement. Josie followed, running all over the Street in her exuberance.

"Well," Edgar Baldwin, a thin dark-haired man said looking at the pieces Abe had laid on the counter. "I ain't never seen nothing like this called gold afore."

four

Abe took in a long breath. When he'd thought the gold was gone he'd felt maybe that was how it was supposed to be. Now that he had it in his hands it had to be gold. Real gold.

Are You there God? he asked silently.

I'm here, Abe.

You'll make sure this is the way You want it, won't You?

Count on it, Abe. And trust Me to know best.

Abe relaxed. Whatever God had in mind was all right with him.

Baldwin looked at the pieces again and shook his head. Finally he called his brother from somewhere in the back. "Waddaya make of this stuff?" he asked.

The bearded man picked up the biggest piece and turned it over several times. "Looks like gold to me. Feels like it too." He set the stone down and looked at Abe. "Where'd you get this stuff?"

Abe grinned. "It came from Idaho but I didn't get it. Some Indians gave it to us. Thought I did 'em a big favor. They think it's gold."

Edgar Baldwin nodded. "I ain't the gold expert in the family. If Dan thinks it's gold, then it's gold." He extended his hand across the counter. "Congratulations, Abe."

"Thanks," Abe said, shaking the hand. "But we want to know how much this stuff's worth."

Dan Baldwin looked over the gold again. "Looks to me like that chunk'd make ten big nuggets. Looks like good stuff too. Might be worth a thousand dollars but I'm not a gold trader."

Abe almost quit breathing. That rock on the counter was only one of dozens they'd brought home. "Where'll I find out for sure? How do we turn this stuff into somethin' we can use?"

Baldwin pointed east. "There's a gold trader on the other side of the Street down about six buildin's. He can help you."

People milled all over the Street, making it hard for Abe and Martha to find the building they sought. Abe had thought the town grew a lot last year, but now the mass of people utterly amazed him. Still all the buildings looked like shacks.

"This here's good gold," the roughly dressed gold expert told them when they found him. "I'll just cut it into small and large nuggets for you. All's I have to do is make all the nuggets weigh the same. If'n you want you can trade the smaller pieces on nuggets."

Abe felt as if he were glowing. "Sounds great. How much you planning to charge for all this?"

The man shrugged. "I can take ten percent. Or I can take the stuff that's too small to weigh. Whatever you say."

Abe looked at Martha, who just smiled at him. "What do I know about these things?" she asked.

"I guess we'll think a little on it," Abe said, turning toward the rough wood door. "We'll be back soon."

☙

When they closed their own door at home, Abe grabbed Martha high in his arms and twirled her around. "We're rich!" he shouted. "Positively, absolutely rich! And so are all our kin."

After they collected Willie from Aunt Mandy and ate dinner, they sat on the settle and talked. "Let's count the pieces of gold and see if we can tell how much we have," Abe said. They hauled the three heavy sacks of gold from their hiding places and counted the big pieces, guessing how many big nuggets could be cut from each. They did the same with the smaller pieces. When they finished, Abe looked at Martha. Her eyes reflected his shock. They'd tried to be conservative with their estimates, but they figured they'd have more than fifty thousand dollars.

"We don't need that much money," Abe said. "With all the new people comin' in I can make a good living makin' furniture. And we can make a living from our farm too."

"We do need it, Abe," Martha said quietly. "We purely do. We can do a lot of good with it. I hear they're trying to get a school going right away. We can help that. And all kinds of other things too." She giggled. "We might even help my brother a little."

Abe laughed with her. "We'll help him a little, but he has to learn to work like other men. We'll also help your aunt and uncle. And Riley and Melissa." Martha's cousin, Riley, had married Melissa, who'd lived with Martha and Abe since Martha had found her hungry and frightened, looking in the window. Although scarcely a year younger than Martha, Melissa considered Martha and Abe her parents. "We mustn't forget God, either," Abe added. "The Good Book says to give Him a tenth of our increase. But that ain't enough. We'll give more like we always have." He chuckled. "That much gold may puzzle our church brothers a bit."

"Will we take all the money to the gold trader? Or a little at a time?"

Abe took her hand in his. "I don't think we'll do exactly either. Let's take several pieces right away and share with your kin, the school, the church, and whatever. Then we can get it fixed up as we or someone needs it."

That afternoon they took a bag of larger pieces to the gold man who cut them into nuggets. He kept the small pieces he cut off for his payment.

They took ten big nuggets to Aunt Mandy and Uncle Cleve.

"Oh, honey," Uncle Cleve said in his usual bellow. "We don't need them. We have plenty left to live until our crops mature. Riley and Melissa won't need any either. He had several big nuggets just the other day. And they put in lots of crops."

"Well," Abe said as they crossed the creek toward their place, "we didn't get rid of even one nugget." He grinned. "Jackson won't turn us down. But right now why don't we take this bag of nuggets to the new school? I hear they're plannin' to open next month. I'm thinkin' they could use the money now. Then let's walk out to Fort Walla Walla and buy us each a saddle horse. We might even find a cow. People been drivin' them in from California already."

Willie rode Speck along as they walked first to the school, then the two miles to the fort. "What kind of horse you gonna get, Martha?" he asked.

Martha laughed. "I don't know, Willie. Whatever they have, I guess." She sobered. "I can't expect another Sampson. Or even close. He was one of a kind." Her beloved chestnut gelding, Sampson, froze in the cold last winter.

Abe took her hand. He knew how she felt. He'd lost his treasured mare, Charity, just before the cold. When he'd gone to California to buy and drive cattle home, Indians had stolen Charity and eaten her. It still made his stomach churn to remember.

Soon they reached the fort and a soldier took them to the log corral where they kept the horses they wanted to sell.

Abe spotted *the horse* before he'd looked at half the herd, a huge black stallion with a perfect star in its forehead. White covered all four feet like knee stockings.

Whaddaya say, Father? he asked silently. *Would You be for me havin' that one?*

He looks good, Abe.

All right! Thanks, Pard.

But Abe wouldn't say anything until Martha chose. She came first and Sampson had been big. She might choose that big black beauty by the fence. He tried to look at the other horses before him but his eyes seemed stuck on the black.

"Oh, Abe," Martha said, clutching his arm. "See that pretty little chestnut mare? She looks nearly like Charity. Do you want her?"

Abe shook his head. "Not this time. I wouldn't like being reminded of Charity every day. Have you found one you like?"

"Not yet," Martha said, her eyes shining with excitement and love. "But I'm not choosing until you do."

Abe laughed. "I hope we won't be standin' here all night but you're choosin' first."

Martha laughed too. "All right, Abe, if you're sure." Her eyes turned toward the corral. "See that big big boy over there? That cream-colored gelding?" She turned raptured eyes on Abe. "Oh, Abe, isn't he wondrous?"

"Yeah!" Willie said. "That 'n's just right for a girl." Then he pointed into the middle of the herd. "You gotta take that black one over there, Abe."

Abe ruffled the little boy's blond hair. "Hey, you've been so quiet I thought you'd gone away somewhere." He turned his eyes back to the big black. "You like that one, do you? Well, I might take him—just for you."

When Abe pointed out the cream and black horses, the soldier grinned. "I bin wantin' that black myself," he said. "I bet he'll give you a ride you'll remember." He looked through the sheets of paper he held in his hands. A moment later he looked up. "The black's seven years old and $225. Name's Lucifer."

Abe's eyes quickly met Martha's. She grinned. He didn't.

That name definitely had to go. "How hard you reckon it is on a horse to have his name changed?" Abe asked.

The man shrugged. "Reckon it won't matter none. The horse'll soon come to whatever you call it. Prolly think their name's a call to food anyways." Then he looked up Martha's horse on his paper. "Yer horse is four years old, Ma'am. Prolly got more energy than a tornado. $245. Name's Thunder. 'Course you can change it if you want."

Responding to Abe's question about a cow, the man shook his head. "We ain't got any extra milking right now, but I hear they're coming in by the hunnerds."

As they rode home Abe touched his heels to Lucifer's sides. The horse moved into a nice trot. He touched them again and the horse took off on a rolling canter. He took the slack from the reins and the horse slowed. He leaned over and petted the powerful black neck. "We'll do all right, won't we, boy?" he asked the shiny horse. "I've never seen a more responsive animal. And I'll be buildin' you a good tight barn before winter."

When they neared home, Abe asked Martha, "What do you think? Think you'll get along with Thunder?"

"I love him, Abe. I purely love him. I'm going to find some sugar cubes for him right away."

"I gotta give Speck some too," Willie said. "You know what, Martha? Speck looks a lot smaller than he did before you and Abe got your horses."

Martha laughed. "He may be small but he's a good faithful friend. Now we can take long rides, Willie. When we're together, we won't have to stay in sight of the house."

That night Riley and Melissa stopped by. Abe wandered into his bedroom, returning with a bag of nuggets. "Got somethin' here might help you out some," Abe said, handing the bag to Riley.

Riley opened the bag and looked inside. His gaze jerked

to Abe's over the top of the bag. "What's that all about?" he asked.

Abe grinned and sat down across from Riley and Melissa. "We been prospectin'—well, in a way. The Indians took us after some gold and we figgered that was about your share."

Riley closed the bag and shoved it back toward Abe. "Reckon we don't need it, Abe. Thanks for thinkin' on us anyway. We planted a lot of garden stuff and we're sellin' it as fast as we can haul it to the Street. We got more'n enough to last another year already. And we got over two months left." He looked as if he'd done something mean and felt sorry. Then his lips lifted into a grin. "Reckon Jackson and Nellie could use some though."

Abe grinned back. "That's what I been hearin'. Did they put in any crops? Or anything?"

Riley shook his head. "Not to notice. I think Jackson's been helping build some cabins though."

Martha joined Abe on the settle. "Think he'd keep working if we gave him something?" she asked the men.

"I guess he deserves a chance to show us," Abe said. "We'll have to go give them their share tomorrow."

They decided to go that evening after Riley and Melissa left so they could catch Jackson at home. Besides it would be a good chance to ride the new horses. Abe had been thinking about a name for his horse. "What do you think of Midnight for my horse?" he asked Martha and Willie. "I realize it isn't very original but he's black."

Martha hesitated. "He's black all right. Would you rather have a name that's a little different? I was thinking about King Ebony. Ebony's black, you know. You could call him King. But Midnight's good too, Abe. I was just thinking."

King Ebony. That sounded pretty good. And there wouldn't be half a dozen other horses around with that name.

He grinned. "I think I like that name, Martha. 'Course there' probably a lot of Kings around. Yeah. It's King Ebony. And I'll call him Ebb. Purty classy, huh, Willie?"

"Yeah!" Willie yelled at the top of his lungs. "I like it! Best of all I like for you to have horses again so you can ride with me."

Before they knew it, they reached Jackson and Nellie's place. Jackson gladly accepted the nuggets. "How come you didn't invite us to go?" he asked. "We could have gotten enough to last the rest of our lives."

"The Good Lord knows workin's good for us, Jackson," Abe said kindly. "It strengthens our muscles, our minds, and our morals."

Later, when they crawled into their warm feather bed, Abe held Martha close. "Thanks for thinkin' up Ebb's name," he said. "I love everything about you, includin' your good mind."

Two days later Gray Wolf came to their house alone. And he didn't say "food."

Abe thought Martha's face paled. "What's wrong?" she asked.

"Come talk Indian," he said. "New jail—steal three cows. Not steal cows."

Abe moved over and put his arm over Martha's shoulder. "Let's go," he said quietly. "Want to come, Gray Wolf?"

The Indian followed them to the Street, then west to the building housing the jail. "We'd like to see the Indian who's charged with stealing the cows," Abe said politely.

"Ya mean the Indian what did steal the cows—three of 'em," Sheriff Buckley said smugly. "Guess I can let you see the savage. Don't talk nuthin' but gibberish though." He led the way down a dirty rough-wood walkway, stopping at a big steel cage. "That's him, sittin' on that box." The sheriff turned and hurried back.

Abe turned to Gray Wolf. "You know him?"

Gray Wolf shook his head. "Heard him."

"How do you know he didn't do it?"

"Say so."

Abe grinned. That might be a good enough reason for Gray Wolf, but he doubted the jury would agree. Especially a white jury. "Can you talk to him?" he asked the tall bronze man.

"What say?"

Abe grinned again. "Ask if he took the cows."

The Indian said some Nez Percé words Abe didn't understand and the other one answered.

"Not take cows," Gray Wolf told Abe.

"Do you know when this happened?" Abe asked.

Gray Wolf didn't. Abe went after the sheriff. "We all need to talk this out," he explained. The sheriff came back reluctantly. "When did this happen?" Abe asked.

"Three or four days ago."

"Why do you think the Indian did it?" Abe asked. "Did he have the cows?"

Buckley spit on the floor. "You know better'n that. Them Indians ate the cows right off."

"Tell me about it."

"Them cows disappeart 'bout soon's they arrived from California. They weren't nowhere. If'n a white man got 'em he'd a hung on to 'em for breeding. Only a dumb redskin woulda et 'em when cows're so scarce around here."

Abe began to feel they didn't have a case against the Indian at all. He looked at his boot and wiped it on the back of his overall leg. "But—uh—why do you think it's this particular one?"

For a moment Sheriff Buckley looked concerned. Then he met Abe's eyes and grinned. "Well, I figgered we'd make an example of 'im. Lots a' cows disappearin' lately. We gotta stop it somehow, Abe. After we string up that Injun, won't have much rustlin' no more."

"You know better'n that, Sheriff. You gotta find the guilty man or it'll never stop. If it's a white man he'll be tickled to death for you to keep on throwin' Indians in jail. They'll like it even better if you hang 'em."

The sheriff didn't argue, but led Abe and Gray Wolf to the outside door. "Good-bye," the sheriff said. "See you in court."

"What happen?" Gray Wolf asked.

"You can expect your friend to be released before the day's over," Abe said.

Gray Wolf smiled, something very rare for him. "Thank you, Abe. Need gold?"

Abe held his hand to Gray Wolf, who snatched it and shook hard. "We'll never need more gold," he told his Indian friend. "You gave us enough to last all our lives."

Later that afternoon Abe returned to the sheriff and demanded he release the Indian. Finally the reluctant man unlocked the door and ushered the surprised Indian outside.

❧

"Let's take the horses and ride until we find some cows," Abe suggested to Martha and Willie the next day. "A lot of cattle have been brought in from California, and we have gold—so let's get as many as we can."

As they rode, Abe noticed how settled the area was becoming. Houses were coming up blocks south of the Street, which had expanded east over Mill Creek all the way past their place. Out past the houses, tents littered the landscape.

As they headed west, Willie yelled, "I see lots of cows. Over there by those trees."

Abe followed Willie's finger and sure enough, hundreds of cows grazed on a low hill. "You're right, Willie. No one wants that many cows for himself. Let's go talk to the man."

The cows had arrived from California less than a week earlier and the man was ready to sell. Abe bought two hundred cows, twenty milking, sixty due to freshen in the next two months, and the rest not bred yet.

"What are we going to do with all that milk?" Martha asked as they rode home.

"Haven't you noticed all the people milling around?" Abe asked, grinning happily. "We'll sell the milk. I just had a thought, though. Remember my little wife a few years ago? And Melissa a little later? I'll bet there's lots of hungry people around. Maybe we could figure out a way to find them and give them food. With the crowd we have around now it might not be so easy."

"I'd love to, Abe," Martha said. "I'd purely love to. I'd be happy to use all our gold feeding hungry people. I remember how awful it is. But how are you going to get those cows out of that herd and drive them home?"

"I was thinkin' about gettin' Riley and Jackson to help me."

"Abram Noble! You have Willie and me. We're two people on two horses. Why can't we help?"

Abe's heart grew large. What a woman. She'd do anything for him, whether she could or not. But maybe she could. He took the slack from Ebb's reins. "Want to try it now? The pasture fences are still good."

Martha wanted to and Willie *really* wanted to, so they turned around and went back. With the help of the rancher and his sons they got the cattle separated from the herd and started theirs back to their farm. The rancher and his sons rode along with them.

About halfway home the cattle decided to break away, running in all directions. "Hup!" the rancher yelled. "We're losing 'em all!"

five

Everyone turned his horse to head off the cattle nearest him. The rancher and his sons regrouped the majority, Martha and Thunder got their share, and Willie gathered in several too. Abe and Ebb raced around and turned the remaining few back southeast. Finally the cows quieted down and plodded along within the ring of riders on three sides of them.

"Hey, Willie," Abe called, "you're a natural born cowboy. You did almost better'n anyone. Next to Martha, of course."

"Yippee!" Willie yelled, "I'm gonna be a cowboy. Speck's gonna be my horse too."

They got the cows into the pasture with no more trouble.

Martha went into the house while Abe and Willie took care of the horses. She felt exhilarated too. Bringing the cows home seemed like a great accomplishment. Giggling to herself, she decided maybe she'd be a cowboy too when she grew up. Her heart grew almost too big for her chest as she thought about Abe. He always knew just the right thing to say to make Willie proud. She hurried to get supper ready for her boys.

Later the Indians came and ate some of Martha's fresh bread while she taught them about Jesus' love.

The next morning Abe went out to check on the new cattle and make sure they found the creek, while Martha did the washing and started bread. She'd just filled the tub with hot water when Abe came rushing in.

"Fifty of the cows are gone," he said. "Can you get Thunder and help me look for them?"

Martha dropped the clothes she'd been sorting, called Willie, and went out with Abe.

"You and Willie go east and I'll go west," he said. "They can't be far."

They searched fruitlessly most of the day, then met back at their place. "I'm afraid they didn't wander off," Abe said. "They'd never go that far."

"What do you mean?" Martha asked. "You don't think someone took them!"

Abe grinned with only a trace of sadness in his face. "I'm afraid we just lost a big hunk of yesterday's investment." He went to finish caring for the remaining livestock, the two big work horses, and the three saddle horses.

Martha returned to her ruined bread and unwashed clothes. *Oh well,* she told herself, *there's always tomorrow.* She made baking powder biscuits and split pea soup.

The next day Abe had to go to the Street so Martha set bread again and heated water for washing. She'd finished with the bread, put it in the warming oven to rise, and was scrubbing sheets when he came back excited.

"Two stores were burglarized last night and they tell me it's happening all the time."

Martha straightened from the scrub board and rubbed her back. "What does Sheriff Buckley think about it?"

Abe grimaced. "The same thing he always does. Says an Indian did it. That might be true, but it might not." He dropped into a chair beside the table. "Somethin's gotta be done, Martha. It's gettin' so nuthin' and nobody's safe around here." He bowed his head. "Lord, You gotta show me what to do. All right?"

He sat with his head bowed awhile, then looked at Martha

with a grin. "He says if the law won't stop it the rest of us got to."

Two days later the man they had bought the cattle from appeared at their door. Martha invited him in and gave him a glass of cool milk and some oatmeal cookies while Willie ran to get Abe from the barn.

After Abe washed up a little he shook the man's hand. "Glad to see you. Maybe you heard I need some more cows?"

The man shook his grizzled gray head. "I didn't. In fact, I came to see if you'd come after some while I wasn't lookin'."

Abe looked shocked. "You don't mean you wondered if I stole 'em? I didn't, sir. How many'd you lose?"

"About as many as you bought as near as I can figger. It looked like I had a lot of cattle, but I spent everthin' I had on them critters and I needed the money bad."

Abe looked pained. "Know of anyone else who's lost animals?"

The man laughed mirthlessly. "Yeah. Everone you talk to. Sometimes stuff disappears. Other times masked robbers get it with guns. 'Pears to me this town's getting outta control."

"Me too," Abe agreed. "I lost a bunch too. Let's watch close-like awhile and try to get Buckley interested in cleanin' up Walla Walla. Used to be you could leave a nugget in the street and it'd be there when you got back."

Abe checked his cattle often and cared for them carefully to be sure they got plenty of food and water. He hired three men to help milk and sold twenty-five gallons of milk every day. He gave away about the same amount. He'd put up a sign on McMorris's general store for anyone who couldn't buy milk and needed it to come to their place. Martha gave milk to everyone who came. All they had to bring was their own bottles, jugs, or cans.

Soon people began getting robbed on the Street. Many times the robbers injured their victims and sometimes killed them. No one was safe, not even the strongest of men. Even the merchants weren't safe. Several of the newer businesses gave up after numerous robberies.

Fifty more of Abe's cows disappeared one night, leaving him with half what he'd bought. The same thing happened to all the settlers, and discontent increased to a crescendo.

When they tried to talk to Sheriff Buckley, he simply shrugged. "You seen all those people milling up and down the street? And the hunnerds of tents nearby? I got two marshals 'n that's all. What's three men gonna do in that mess? I'll tell you what they're gonna do. They're gonna get 'emselves killed. That's what." So he sat in his office and listened to complaints.

A month later seven more businesses folded. Others hired armed men to watch over them while they continued serving the public. Several people died defending their goods or themselves.

Late one night Josie erupted like a spring from the floor where she'd been sleeping. The hair on the back of her neck stood up and a low growl rumbled deep in her throat. "Shhhh," Martha whispered to the big dog. "What do you hear, Josie?" Then Martha heard a loud buzz, like many people talking and stomping around. A loud pounding on the door brought both her and Abe to their feet.

"Are you going to open the door?" Martha asked, feeling herself start to shake. "They're going to wake Willie in a minute."

Abe, who'd been reading *The Statesman* with Martha, grinned. "As many as 're out there, they'll knock the door down if we don't."

Martha peered around him as he threw open the door. She couldn't believe how many men stood out there. Maybe a hundred. "Come on out, Abe," McMorris yelled. "We're forming a vigilance committee to clean up this town and we need you."

"I better see what's happening," he told Martha. "Lock the door behind me." He stepped out into the black night, and she turned the block of wood to lock the door.

Martha sat back down and tried to read the paper but after reading a shocking article about people selling babies, she couldn't remember one thing she'd read. "Please take care of Abe, God," she prayed out loud. "He's so good and can do so much good for You. And I purely love him, Lord." She giggled ever so quietly. "But You love him even more, don't You? Thank You, Father. I could never get by one day without You."

She mended some overalls for Willie, hugged and petted Josie because the men had made her nervous, swept the floor, hugged and encouraged Josie, prayed for Abe's safety, hugged and loved Josie. "I'm getting tired," she told the faithful dog, "but I'm not going to bed until Abe comes home safely."

Sometime after midnight a soft knock on the door awakened Martha from the settle where she'd fallen asleep. She crept to the door. "Who is it?" she whispered, hoping if it wasn't Abe, the person wouldn't be able to tell she was a woman.

"It's me," Abe's dear voice called. "I promise not to eat you alive."

When she fumbled the lock open, he came in looking excited. "We're going to stop this lawlessness," he said. Then he chuckled. "Looks like my job is to keep anyone from gettin' killed. I mean the thieves 'n rustlers. Those boys are right mad."

A cold fear stabbed Martha. "How can a bunch of you stop them when the sheriff can't?"

Abe took her hand. "You just said it, Martha. That was a big bunch here tonight. We're gonna meet again tomorrow night to get organized. Then we'll divide up and watch this town day and night. We won't take the bounders to Buckley. We'll just figger out our own justice, somethin' that'll make 'em sorry fer what they did."

Martha felt fear again. "You aren't going to be a criminal in order to catch criminals, are you, Abe?"

He grinned and shook his head. "I told you that's my job. Somehow we gotta get the job done but I gotta keep 'em under control. Let's go to bed, Martha. I have a strong feelin' tomorrow's gonna be a big day."

Willie woke at dawn next morning and wanted Martha to ride with him. They quietly left the house in order not to awaken Abe, saddled Speck and Thunder, and took off. Somehow, before the sun came over the Blue Mountains, they ended up several miles south of town, over some rolling hills.

Suddenly Willie pointed south. "Look, Martha. Look at those men herding all those cows. Are they cowboys like me, Martha? Are they?"

When Martha saw the six or eight men driving a large herd of cattle toward the mountains, her heart jumped into her throat. Were those men legally moving the cattle?

"I'm not sure, sweet," she answered calmly. "Say, I'll bet Abe's awake and hungry. I'll race you home, Willie." She loosened Thunder's reins but didn't give him his head.

The big horse would leave Willie and Speck in the dust and she'd never do that. Better for Willie to think he and Speck at least had a chance.

The horses took off in a fast canter which Speck soon turned into a gallop. That little horse really ran fast for his size. Thunder idled along just ahead of Speck. Martha let them go for awhile, then slowed Thunder to rest Speck.

After a little while they galloped again, then trotted. Finally they reached their place. "Let's get the horses rubbed down fast, Willie," Martha said. "Then you can give them some oats while I fix breakfast."

Abe was up and dressed when Martha rushed through the door—thankfully without Willie. "I might have bad news," she burst out as he greeted her with a hug and kiss. She told him about the cattle and riders heading toward the Blues.

"Were they pushing the cattle hard?" Abe asked.

"I don't know, Abe. I just hurried back to tell you."

"I'll gather up whoever I can and go after them," he said. "This may be exactly what we're hopin' for. Can you get breakfast ready while I'm gone?" He took off out the door without waiting for an answer.

Martha put some potatoes on to fry with bacon cut through them. Then she made hot biscuits. The least she could do would be to send him away with a full stomach. He might not get any dinner.

Abe returned and while he ate, he told Martha as much of his plans as he could with Willie sitting there.

"I got Cleave, Riley, Jackson, and six of the men who came after me last night. We're goin' for a ride." He chuckled. "I got our kin cause I figgered they won't lose their heads."

Abe kissed Martha good-bye and tousled Willie's soft hair.

"I'll hurry back," he said. "Quick as we can." He pulled Martha tight to him. "Say a couple of prayers," he whispered against her ear.

Then they disappeared behind the house, heading south. Martha and Willie spent the morning weeding the vegetables. Martha prayed every time she could clear her head from Willie's chattering.

As the afternoon wore on Martha became more and more concerned over Abe. She sent Willie off on several errands so she could pray uninterrupted.

Just as Martha started preparing supper she heard a great commotion in the yard. "Martha, Abe's here," Willie called.

She dropped a potato on the table and ran outside. One look at Abe's dejected face told her things hadn't gone well. "What happened?" she asked.

He talked as he rubbed Ebb down. "This here's some horse," he said. "He's all heart. Really worked him today. Never found 'em, Martha. We found a lot of tracks but they sort of disappeared in the grass."

Martha hurt for him. "Are you convinced they were stolen cattle?"

He nodded. "Tomorrow I'll try to find the owner. He might be a big help to us."

Abe disappeared to care for the livestock. Martha finished supper.

The next day Abe invited Martha and Willie to ride to the far out places with him. They left right after breakfast and Abe stopped at every place that looked as if it had or could handle cattle. Most said they had cattle coming from California, Texas, or Mexico. Some had lost all their cattle in the cold and didn't want anymore.

Finally they found their man. His anger spilled over Abe,

Martha, and Willie when they approached him. "Yes, I lost a lot of cattle. Night before last. What do you know about it, young man? Are you looking for more?"

Abe didn't blink. "No sir, I'm trying to find the men who're rustlin' and bring them to justice. How long had you had your cattle, sir?"

"Three days. Not even long enough to get them settled down. Just brung 'em from Texas. Fine bunch of cattle. Disappeared the second night we had 'em. If I find the perpetrators I'll take the law into my own hands. They don't deserve no pussyfoot handlin' like the sheriff hands out."

"We've just formed a vigilance committee, sir. Would you like to join?"

For the first time the man appeared interested in Abe. He looked him over. "Who are you, anyway, son? Are you from the law?"

Abe grinned. "Not so's you'd notice. A bunch of us decided to forget the law and clean up our part of the world. Get rid of the rustlers, and the sticky fingers in town."

"You bet! I'd like to help do that."

"All right! We're meeting at my place tonight at dusk. Be there." Abe told the man how to get to his place, took the man's name, and the little group rode off. "I wish we'd found the man's cattle," Abe said.

That night ninety-three people gathered at Abe's place and they sat on the bank of the creek to talk. Martha sat with Abe but didn't take part in the discussion. Feelings ran high as most of the men had lost something personally to the lawless segment. They divided the men into ten groups of nine each and decided where each would guard. Then they discussed how to handle the thieves when they apprehended them.

"I say we shoot 'em on the spot," one young man shouted.

"What we gonna do, help the situation or add to the violence?" Abe asked quietly.

"We gotta give 'em a reason not to do it again," someone else offered.

"Maybe 'pends on what they did," a voice called out. "Flog 'em on the Street for stealin' somethin' worth less than $100. Hang 'em for stealin' cattle or horses or killin' people."

"What about stealin' somethin' worth $500?" a high voice asked.

"Ain't nothin' worth that much but cattle," someone answered.

"Isn't there some way other than hanging?" Abe asked.

Ninety-three jeers told Abe what they thought of his gentle ideas. "If you don't want to restore law and order to this town, why don't you go help the sheriff?" someone called.

"Yeah," someone else added, "we're gonna get rid of this thievin', rustlin', and killin', now, 'stead of after a bunch more of their kind comes in."

"Yeah! We'll let the varmints know this here town's off limits to the likes of them."

The meeting ended with each group starting their watch. Part sleeping the other watching.

As Abe and Martha prepared for their Bible reading and prayer they talked about the meeting. "Guess I was right about havin' to keep things under control," he said. "Some of these boys could end up as honored guest in a necktie party themselves if they don't watch out."

six

Abe fell into bed, dead tired. His group had chosen four men to watch the south side of the Street. Abe volunteered, but they'd informed him they'd start out with real men. Men who really wanted to stop crime.

He turned over in bed, then turned over again. Why did he feel so agitated? Maybe he should get up and check on the men so they wouldn't do something they'd regret.

Sleep, Abe. You can't save the West single-handed. You've done a good work getting this thing started so forget it for tonight. Sometimes drastic sins demand drastic measures. Remember Sodom and Gomorrah? Good night, Abe.

"Thanks, Lord," Abe whispered, feeling a huge load leave his heart. Why hadn't he handed it over to God in the beginning? "Thanks again, Father," he whispered. "You'll be doin' a better job watchin' than I would, won't You? And You don't need sleep. Good night, Father." He leaned over and kissed Martha's sweet sleeping lips, and fell into a sound sleep.

The next morning Abe told Martha what the Lord had said to him.

"Do you think that means there's going to be bloodshed over this?" Martha asked.

"I'm sure," Abe said. "When men find an easy way to get rich quick they don't quit just because someone asks them to."

As soon as Abe and his three helpers got through with his

chores he headed for the Street to see if anything had happened. Not seeing anything, he hurried to the home of one of the men who'd been on duty. "Hey, Abe, come on in," the man said. "Wait'll you hear what happened. Someone caught some cattle rustlers red-handed. If you ride out south a ways you might see four varmints swingin' in a tree. Now, I ain't no idee who could a done it, but those boys won't be doin' nuthin' again fer a long long time."

Abe felt his breakfast coming up and tore out the door. Outside, he fell to his knees, then sat on the ground, feeling a little better. "Lord, is this the way You want it to happen?" he asked.

You're all right Abe. Get up and go home.

Abe didn't wait to ask the man if anything had happened on the Street. He and Martha walked downtown later in the day and everyone had heard about the hanging. All were shocked, but most rejoiced, hoping this would slow the violence that seemed to escalate every day.

Abe worked with Martha in the vegetable gardens that day.

That night Abe joined the group watching the Street. They'd decided to have all nine men working together in each group for safety. Four patrolled each end of the Street and one watched near the center. They walked and talked quietly for hours, taking turns waiting in the center. Just before dawn all Abe could think about was getting through and hitting the bed for a couple of hours.

Abe, you need to be alert. Look around.

Suddenly Abe didn't feel even a little sleepy. "Come on," he said softly to the others, "let's pick up our pace a little. No telling what'll happen around here before mornin'."

Less than fifteen minutes later Abe saw a movement at the side of the gold expert's place. He pointed silently and all four moved toward the building. The man seemed to be leaving the place. Abe and another man dashed around the building so they could corner him between the buildings, two on each side.

"Stop right where you are!" Abe yelled when they were all in place. "We're a posse and we're armed. Don't move or reach for anything!"

The man's hands flew into the air.

Slowly the group of men closed in until they circled him, just out of reach. "State your name and what your business is here at this time of night."

"I'm Joseph Winieke. I own this place and decided to check on it. What do you think you're doing?"

Abe peered through the near-darkness. Sure enough, it was the man who'd taken care of their gold. "He's right, boys," Abe said. "Relax." He turned to Winieke. "Sorry, sir. We're a group of men who've decided to watch the town and try to curb the violence. Do you realize it's not safe for you to come to the Street alone in the night?"

"I know. That's why I'm here checking my place."

With unspoken agreement, the men rushed away from the man's place of business and headed off down the street. "That was purty embarrassin'," one of the men said.

Nothing more happened so when day broke they all went home. As Abe hurried home, he grumbled. "Now why did You tell me to wake up, God? You figger I needed to be embarrassed a little?"

No, Abe, I figgered if you were wide awake you could prevent a terrible accident—and you did.

Abe felt properly chastised for scolding God. "Sorry, Father. I had no call to holler at You. I know you don't make mistakes." He grinned. "But I sure do."

As far as Abe could find, nothing had happened in any of the patrols that night. He slept until about ten o'clock, got up, and helped Martha in the vegetable gardens.

Just before they quit working for dinner, Jackson and Nellie rode in from the back. "We got lots of news," Jackson said. "Nellie gets to tell hers first."

Nellie blushed and her hand fluttered to her stomach. "Well, Jackson and I are going to have a baby early next year." Her eyes flitted from Abe to Martha and back. "I hope you're glad."

Martha jumped up and hugged her. "Of course we're glad. I'm purely thrilled to death, Nellie."

Abe put his arm over her shoulder. "I'm glad too, Nellie. Maybe a little jealous." He dropped his other arm over Martha and pulled her close. "I'm just a hopin' we'll be next."

Nellie laughed out loud and threw her arms around both Martha and Abe. "Oh, thank you, thank you," she said. "I was scared you'd be mad about the baby, 'cause Jackson doesn't work like he should."

Abe laughed. "That's between the two of you, Nellie. Maybe the baby will make him feel more responsible and he'll get to work."

"I'm goin' to," Jackson said. "I'm goin' to even before it's born." He chuckled. "'Course them nuggets you gave us'll last a long time."

Abe shook his head. "Not as long as you might think. Better save them for emergencies."

Martha fixed potato soup for everyone before going back to work. Abe felt proud of her. He'd been wanting bad to start their family but hesitated to mention it to her for fear she'd think he was complaining. He sighed. It would just have to happen when it happened.

After supper that evening, Martha and Abe read *The Statesman* for a little while before Abe had to leave. They laughed at an announcement that said the men at the mines who subscribed to the paper shouldn't dilute their gold dust with sand when they paid. It also said that the school opened July 10 with fifty-seven pupils, and due to a generous benefactor was doing exceptionally well.

When darkness covered the world again, Abe kissed Martha and Willie good-bye and headed for the Street. The night passed quietly and Abe hurried home. He'd eat breakfast, take care of the animals, and go to bed for awhile.

After feeding the horses, he hurried out to the cows in the pasture. But they weren't there! He walked around awhile searching, then admitted the cows had disappeared. A hundred and fifty cows rustled while he watched the Street! That was not only a big loss but a huge insult. Now he was mad enough to string up the rustlers himself—well maybe not. He hoped not anyway.

"What do I do now, Lord? Go after those vermin?"

You're doing fine, Abe. Keep up the good work.

"I don't feel like I'm doing fine, Lord. What are we supposed to do for milk now? And those cows were going to start a big herd for us. I sort of pictured a large Noble dairy in a couple of years."

Don't worry about tomorrow, Abe. Why don't you get one cow to provide your milk right now? You take care of Martha and Willie today. I'll worry about your tomorrows.

"Thanks, Lord," Abe said. Then he wondered if that thanks had been a tiny bit sarcastic. He'd better go tell Martha what happened. She had to find out.

"You men will get this town all straightened out soon," Martha said when he told her. "Then we can have all the cows we want."

That afternoon Abe rode around looking for anyone with cows. Seemed there weren't very many anymore. When he came to a place with seven cows he stopped to ask.

"Last week I got home from drivin' three hundred head of cattle from California," the man said. "Long hard trip. Two nights ago someone walked off with the whole herd. I can tell you I was mighty glad to see those rustlers swinging on the end of a rope, even though they weren't the ones got mine. Hope whoever strung 'em up gets the ones got mine."

Abe almost told the man he thoroughly agreed with his thinking. *Better not.* "Would you like to join a group of citizens trying to cut out crime?"

The man wanted to so Abe told him to come to his house at dusk.

That night nearly one hundred and fifty men showed up at the meeting. Abe stood before the group. "You all here to stamp out crime?" he called.

A mighty roar answered him so they divided into fifteen groups, hoping to completely cover the near area. As dark descended, each group went to its assigned post.

That night Abe's group apprehended two youths hauling booze out of Galbraith's saloon. Part of the group detained the young men, while the rest put back the dozen bottles of whiskey and nailed the place shut for security.

"Know what happens to people like you?" Abe asked the boys. They both shook their heads, barely visible in the dark. "You get a public beating tomorrow morning at ten o'clock." Even in the dark he saw the youngest one wilt.

The committee didn't turn the boys over to the sheriff, but held them themselves. And promptly at ten o'clock Galbraith himself administered seven lashes with an ox whip to each one. "Yer lucky you ain't on that tree south of town," someone yelled as the victims limped away. "I seen three more carcasses on it this mornin'."

Abe hurried to his friend, one of the group who watched the farms south of town. "Yeah, we got another batch," the man said. "Caught 'em with couple hunnerd cattle headed fer the Blues. Almost made it too. If'n we was to go up there we might find a lot more'n we expect."

"Let's go," Abe said. "Let's get a lot of men and go after them."

They didn't go at that time so Abe went home for a little sleep. About the time he woke up, Sheriff Buckley arrived looking upset. "I want to know what's going on," he told Abe. "Looks to me like things are gettin' out of hand."

Abe grinned. "'Pears to me things've been out of hand for some time now. Everyone who's gotten cattle this summer's lost it again."

The sheriff fidgeted from one foot to the other. "However that may be, I was wonderin' if you know who's taking the law into their own hands."

"Would you like to sit, Sheriff? Right there on that chair." Abe thought for a moment. He'd never tell Buckley anything, yet he didn't want to appear rude. "If I knew for sure, I'd have to thank them. Those varmints got two hundred cattle from me and I didn't like that too much. What you plannin' to do about all this?"

The big whiskery man shook his head. "It's tough, Abe. I ain't got no help—only the city marshals. No tellin' how many people 'er out there wreckin' our town. What can one man do?"

Abe rubbed his clean-shaven chin. "Well, you might find out who's workin' for you and join 'em."

After muttering a few more excuses, the man left. Abe felt so good he jumped into the air, stretching his arms high. They'd clean this town up whether the sheriff liked it or not. He cut three thick slices of fresh homemade bread and spread strawberry jam over them. Ummmm. He'd never tasted better bread—or jam. What would he ever do without his own little Martha? She was everything any man could want and more.

He hurried out to tell her about the sheriff's visit.

ン

In the next weeks thirty-three more bodies appeared on the "Hanging Tree" south of Walla Walla, and 217 people received beatings. Three were young girls and no one complained when Galbraith gave them only two light lashes each with the ox whip.

Not one of the patrols caught anyone for over a week. Abe found and bought fifty cows, ten milking and the others not yet bred. He hired only one man to help milk the ten. The new livestock stayed where they belonged and no one reported anything missing. Abe began to feel pretty good. "Whattaya think, Lord? We about got it licked? How much longer should we keep our vigilance committee on duty?"

Always be vigilante, Abe. About everything.

"What does that mean, Lord? Shall we still watch the town every night? That's purty hard work, Y'know. Missing sleep and all."

Abe didn't receive an answer to his question so decided to let the men decide when to quit.

One afternoon a man and woman walked up to Abe as he helped Martha weed the vegetables. "Hello," he said. "Something I can do for you?"

"I hope so," the friendly-looking man said. "Someone in

one of the stores said you're Abram Noble."

Abe grinned and stuck out his hand. "I reckon someone's right. But no one told me who you are."

The man grinned and his eyes showed a love that few do. "I'm Thomas Dorland and this is my wife, Rachel."

Somehow those names sounded familiar, but Abe couldn't figure out how.

The red headed woman stepped closer to Abe. "I'm Martha's good friend and I can't wait to see her. Can you tell me where she is right now?"

Abe turned to look down toward the end of the garden to find Martha hurrying toward them. The other woman held out her arms and so did Martha. Abe thought they'd never turn loose of each other.

Thomas Dorland must have thought so too, for he stepped to the women's side. "Martha, remember me? I'm Tom."

Martha and Rachel pulled apart, and Martha held her hand to Tom. "I'm so glad to see you both," she said. "I can't tell you how many times I've dreamed about you, Rachel. I've missed you terribly. But whatever are you doing here?"

Tom laughed. "We're looking for a place to live—and set up business. Got any ideas?"

seven

"You mean here?" Martha asked, her eyes large with surprise. "I thought you settled in Oregon City." Then her eyes glowed with understanding. She threw her arms around Rachel again. "Yes! You have to settle right here in Walla Walla and doctor our people." Martha couldn't believe her eyes and ears. Rachel was going to be near and be her friend again. She hugged Rachel again. "I can't remember ever being so happy to see anyone before. I purely can't." Then her eyes met Abe's. He looked amused.

"Except when Abe went to California. I'm sorry, Abe. I must make you acquainted. Rachel this is the most perfect, wonderful, handsome husband in the world—mine. Abe meet my dearest friend, Rachel Butler—I guess it's Dorland now. And her husband, Tom. He's a doctor, Abe. A doctor who really cares."

Abe and Tom shook hands. "You lookin' for a donation land claim, Dr. Dorland?" Abe asked.

Tom shook his head. "I never seem to have time to work ground, Abe. And call me Tom. Everyone else does." He shifted his weight from one foot to another and pulled Rachel close. "We just need a little place to build a house with room for an office." He looked around. "Where's Josie, Martha? She's one of my favorite patients. I hope you still have her."

Martha looked around. "She's fine, probably sleeping in the shade of the house. We'll see her soon." Then Martha remembered their lots on the Street. "They could have one of our lots, couldn't they, Abe? Seems we're never going to use them." Her heart felt so light it might lift her from the ground. "I guess you don't have any children?" she asked Rachel.

Rachel and Tom both laughed. "I guess we do," Tom said. "We have a little boy twenty-one months old and nine-month-old twin boys." He nodded meaningfully. "Yes, Martha, we have children."

"What about you two?" Rachel asked. "I'll bet you can't beat our record."

Martha shook her head, feeling embarrassed. "We don't have any yet. We're just waiting for the Lord to start sending them."

"Yes," Abe agreed. "We'll take all we can get." Suddenly he looked at Martha. "What are we doin', keeping these people out here in the hot sun? You folks come on in and we'll give you a cold drink of water—or milk."

Neither Rachel nor Tom moved to follow Abe and Martha. "Come on," Martha called. "You must be thirsty—or hungry."

"Truth is," Tom said, "we have quite a crew with us. Not only our three young'uns, but Rachel's father. Do you remember Nate Butler, Martha?"

"Of course I do." Martha felt a strange lump in her throat. Tom hadn't mentioned Rachel's mother. "Bring him along. He's probably thirsty too. What about your mother, Rachel?"

"She died when we first got to Oregon City. But we also have a woman with two children and an older woman who insisted on coming too."

This began to sound like a bunch of people. "Oh. . .well, bring them all. We have lots of milk right now. I can make sandwiches, too, if you're hungry."

After asking if Martha was sure, the two left to bring back everyone. They arrived with several wagons and tired oxen an hour later. Abe hurried to help put the wagons in a convenient place and to care for the oxen.

Tom and Josie found each other, both acting as if they'd finally found their dearest friend. Tom had saved Josie's life on the Trail when coyotes tore her stomach open and her intestines nearly out.

Martha invited them in and took the oldest baby, Tommy. She loved the three babies on sight. She'd just love Rachel's babies until God sent her one of her own. Two larger children raced around as if they'd been confined for a long time. Martha knew better, for she'd walked all the way across the country with Willie.

"These two are Joel and Evie," Rachel told Martha. "Joel's six and Evie's three. They've been our best travelers." A dark plump pretty woman approached and stood beside Rachel. "And this is their mother, Melissa Witlow. Her husband was killed in an accident so she lives with us. She's been my lifesaver on the trip and several months before."

Mr. Butler looked just as he'd looked on the Trail, but much happier than Martha expected. She rushed into his arms and he held her tight. "Little Martha," he said softly. He turned to Abe. "I hope you know what a wonderful person this little girl is. She brightened our long hard pilgrimage more than anyone else."

"I know," Abe said. "She brightens my life all day every day." He raised his eyes upward. *Thank You again, God. Only You could have given me a wife like Martha.*

Mr. Butler started, looking around. "Where's Cindy?" he asked Rachel. "Martha has to meet her."

"I'm here, Nate." A petite gray-haired woman dashed up to Mr. Butler, slid under his arm as if she belonged there, and held a hand to Martha. "I'm Cynthia Buchanan—I mean Butler." She looked up at Nate with eyes filled with love. "We're newlyweds," she explained. "We got married on the way. We stopped in the Dalles to rest after that horrible Barlow Road—" She giggled like a young girl. "And ended up married." The woman looked so happy and sweet that Martha couldn't resist hugging her.

After giving them all milk to drink, she started fixing supper. They must be hungry.

"Why don't we walk over to the Street and have a look at our lots?" Abe suggested when he returned from caring for the animals. "If you're interested in one of them, we might as well get going on your house and office. We can build a log buildin' or outta boards, whatever you want. We have a sash factory now and several lumber companies. I 'spect we can have your home and office built in three weeks."

Martha decided supper could wait. She hadn't started anything cooking yet so it wouldn't burn.

Tom didn't seem too excited about the lots on the Street.

"I guess those lots weren't what you had in mind," Abe said as they started back to the house.

Tom grinned ruefully and shook his head. "We thought Walla Walla would be primitive and in a way it is, but I can't believe all the people! More people crowd the Street than we had on our main street in Oregon City."

The group walked on. "The gold frenzy in OroFino caused the population explosion here," Martha explained. "They're all here to cash in on that in one way or another."

When they reached home, Rachel and Melissa helped Martha cook some steaks, potatoes, gravy, beets, and beet greens, with applesauce for dessert. She also served thick slices of homemade bread with lots of butter.

After they finished they talked in the main room. "Do you have many doctors here?" Tom asked. "And do you know anything about their practices?"

Abe shook his head. "We know there are some because they advertise in *The Statesman*, our newspaper, but we've never gone to a doctor. We never needed one—thanks, Lord." He got up, picked up a newspaper and handed it to Tom. "This might help you know what's out there. You can keep it if you'd like."

After a bit the newcomers returned to their wagons for the night.

The next morning, Abe and Martha both milked and cared for the cows, and Abe hauled milk to the Street where he sold it. Then the people began coming for free milk. Martha had given away twelve gallons when Rachel came into the house.

"Are you selling milk from your house?" she asked.

"No, we're giving it away. What we can't give away, we sell."

Rachel seemed unable to understand. "How can you afford to do that?" she asked. "Isn't that the way you make your living?"

Martha felt really good about what they were doing, but felt it better not to tell anyone about the gold. "We've had some wonderful blessings so we're sharing. That's all."

As the group ate breakfast, Tom looked at Rachel. She cleared her throat. "Tom's trying to get me to ask something for him. We talked last night and we'd like a little more land than the lot you showed us. We'd also like a little more quiet. We wondered if you could sell us an acre of your land somewhere near the front?"

Martha looked at Abe who shook his head. "Sorry, Tom. This is a donation land claim and we can't sell any until we've lived on it long enough to satisfy the government." He thought a moment. "We might be able to build you a house and office though. We could fence it off so it would be separate, but it would still have to be in our name."

"Hey! That sounds great to me. We could rent it. What do you think, Angel?" Tom asked Rachel.

She nodded. "I don't care, just so I get to be close to Martha."

"Let's get to work then," Abe said. "But you won't rent it. It'll just be yours. I guess we can help our new doctor that much."

The men left to start planning the new building project and the women cleaned up the dishes and children.

When they'd nearly finished, Nate Butler appeared. "Are you about through with my wife?" he asked. "I'm missing her."

Cynthia rushed into his arms. She giggled softly. "Aren't you embarrassed to act like this in front of the ladies?"

As he shook his dark but graying head, Martha thought his soft blue eyes looked terribly kind, even more than she remembered. "How can I be ashamed?" he asked his new little wife, "when I'm so proud to call you mine?" Holding Cynthia close he turned to Martha. "Cindy and I decided we'd like to take out a donation claim. Think we'd be eligible?"

Martha assured him they would. "Would you like me to take you to the office? But that's getting it backwards. First you find the place you want, then go in. It takes only a few minutes and the place will be yours."

The two hurried away, arm in arm.

"Where did your father ever find someone like that? So sweet? And also so healthy?" Martha asked.

Rachel and Melissa broke into laughter. "You're looking at the world's best fool for God," Melissa said. "Cynthia was brought to Tom and Rachel to care for while she was sick. She was the last straw in a big haystack of people Rachel and Tom took in." Melissa laughed merrily. "They decided to leave to get away from all of us, but Cynthia and I refused to be left behind."

Rachel laughed with her. "She's not quite right. We waited to go until the rest of the children left us and until Tom's patients got well. We didn't leave anyone needing us— except Mrs. Gump." At that name the girls both burst into laughter again.

"Mrs. Gump is a human vulture," Melissa said. "When you see her coming, get out of the way. Rachel had a sewing machine and that woman brought her a trunk of cloth to sew into clothes every week. Even the week the twins were born."

When they had finished the dishes and swept the floor, they sat down in the main room to watch the babies.

Josie insisted on staying beside the little ones, licking their faces and keeping them in the back of the room. When Gabriel and Jesse grabbed her fur and pulled up beside her, she stood still as if she knew they weren't steady on their feet.

Soon Tom and Abe came in. "We have it all staked out, Angel," Tom said. "We'll have a house of our own soon."

Then Nate and Cynthia returned. "The places close in are all taken," Nate said. "We need to be near. Besides we wanted to be close to all of you."

Abe nodded. "Nothin' left close in all right. Any special

reason you need close in?"

"Yes. I'm a blacksmith and need to be where people can find me. We was wondering if you want to sell that lot or was it just to Tom and Rachel?"

"Funny, I was thinkin' on the same thing," Abe said. He looked at Martha. "What do you think?"

"We'll still have one left," Martha said. "Why not let them have it?"

"All right!" Abe said. "We'll build your place too."

The next weeks were busy for everyone. They decided to build Nate and Cynthia's first, as it would be a quicker job. The children spent their days playing outside with Josie and each other. The women kept food cooked for the men who worked hard on Nate's place.

One afternoon a strange Indian walked into Martha's house. For a moment she felt frightened, then remembered her friends, Gray Wolf and his sons. No one could be nicer or truer. She met the tall bronze man in the middle of the room. "May I help you? Do you need some food?"

"Come," the Indian said. Then he added a bunch of Nez Percé words Martha couldn't understand. She managed to sort out the Indian word for hurt. "Is someone hurt?" she asked.

The Indian nodded and repeated his only English word. "Come."

"I think I better go with him," she told Melissa who was helping her do the washing. "Can you take over here?"

Martha walked one step and ran two to keep up with the tall Indian who hurried toward the Street. She tried to learn more from him but he didn't understand any of her words. She'd thought she understood Nez Percé a little but couldn't make out his words at all.

Following the Indian, Martha ended up at the new jail and went in behind him. The marshall met them. "Stop right there, redskin," the man said gruffly.

The Indian stopped. So did Martha. "What's going on?" she asked the man.

The marshall grinned. "You're the ones who just came in. Whaddaya want?"

Martha looked at the Indian and decided there'd be no help from him. "Have you just brought in an Indian?" she asked.

"We've always just brought in an Indian," the man growled. "This here place is full of 'em. Too bad all they can do is grunt like an animal."

"Let this man take me to the one he knows," Martha pleaded.

The guard stepped back. "Ain't no skin off my nose. Make yerself t'home."

The Indian's black eyes met Martha's. She nodded and he took off down the dark hall. He hurried as if he knew where he was going. Suddenly he stopped in front of one of the steel cages and faced it, standing tall and straight. The person inside could barely be called a man—he wasn't more than fourteen or fifteen years old.

"Hello," Martha ventured. The boy inside said nothing. His eyes looked like those of a trapped animal. She couldn't tell if he didn't understand her or was too frightened to talk. "Can I help you?" she asked. Still nothing. She'd have to try something else. She said hello in the Nez Percé language.

His eyes brightened ever so slightly and he said a few soft words. Martha listened closely and understood two words. *Brave hurt*. Did he hurt someone? She held her hand out in a stay motion to the Indian who had sought her help.

Then she ran to the guard. "Come tell me what this boy is accused of," she said, then ran back.

"Well, that'n's been drinking a lot of firewater—if you know what that is."

"I know," Martha said. "Is that a crime?"

"'Tis with them savages. They go plumb wild."

"What did this one do?" Martha asked.

"Well, some feller who just arrived from California got knocked on the head and his nuggets all stoled. This Injun done it. He soon walked into Ball and Stone Saloon flashing the money around. Soon's the man feels better he can identify the savage."

Martha couldn't believe the man calling this justice. "That's not even circumstantial evidence, sir. Lots of people have nuggets—or money."

The man stood tall and looked down on Martha. "It ain't evidence? Well, how come is it your bunch of vigilantes don't even wait to identify the perpetrator? Just string 'em up without waitin' fer nothing."

For a second Martha felt cornered. Then she remembered what those men did wasn't her responsibility. She smiled at the rough-looking man. "They aren't my vigilantes," she said. "But from what I hear they only do that when they catch the men actually herding the stolen cattle out of the valley."

"I don't see no difference, ma'am."

"Well, I do. Mind if I go back and try to talk to the man again?"

The man dropped to a nearby chair. "Go ahead. It's a free country."

Martha hurried back to the cage, the free Indian following her. "Can you talk to me?" she asked the boy in the cell. He didn't answer. Suddenly she had an idea. "Are you Nez

Percé?" she asked. He shrugged and looked confused.

"Help me help this boy, Father," she prayed out loud. "Help me to understand him before something awful happens to him. Thank You in Jesus' name. I love You. Amen." Suddenly she felt lighter and freer than since she'd come. She turned back to the frightened boy. "Cayuse?" The boy nodded his face, showing joy at this bit of communication.

But she didn't feel very relieved. "Lord, how am I going to understand him when I don't know his language at all?"

Then the boy said something to her. And she understood some of it! Somehow she knew they took his nuggets—his only three nuggets. She smiled at him, held up three fingers, and motioned with both hands for him to keep talking.

He said several more guttural words. He said them over and over. Then somehow she knew he hadn't hurt the man but had seen the man who did. "Thank You, Lord," she cried. "You purely are helping me understand this boy." She reached through the cage and patted him on the arm. "I'll be right back," she said and ran after the jailer again. "This boy didn't do it," she said. "But he saw it happen. He didn't take the nuggets, either, and you'd better give his back to him." She almost added that the man who did it was white, but she couldn't say something she wasn't sure about.

The burly man looked surprised. "You really bin talkin' to 'im, ain't you? How you learn all that Injun stuff, anyhow?"

Martha shook her head. "He's Cayuse and I don't understand their language. You have to turn this boy loose, Mr. Gilliam. I asked God to help and He wouldn't let me understand something untrue."

The man sneered and shook his head. "Too bad God don't stop all the crime around here. But since He don't, I guess we'll have to figger out who done it all by ourselves."

Martha decided to go get Abe from down the street where he was working on Nate Butler's house and blacksmith shop. Men listened to him much better. When she told him what happened, he asked if Gray Wolf would understand the Cayuse boy.

"I'm not sure. Should I get Thunder and go find Gray Wolf?" Abe told her to do that while he went on over to the jail.

eight

As Abe hurried to the jail he shook his head. This town would straighten out a lot sooner if everyone didn't try to lay everything on the Indians. He had no doubt the Indians did some of the things the law accused them of, but it seemed the white men couldn't wait to blame every crime on them.

When Abe entered the rough wood building, the marshall grumbled at him. "That little woman a' yours keeps purty busy, don't she? What she think she can do about this here redskin?"

"Hello. How are you, Marshall Gilliam? Beautiful summer day, don't you think?" Abe ambled down the dark aisle toward the cages where they kept the prisoners. The jailer followed. Soon Abe spotted a tall Indian outside a cell occupied by a very young boy. Looked like it could be father and son. This must be the one.

He turned back to the officer. "Martha tells me you have no reason to hold this young man. She also tells me he didn't do it but knows who did. Why don't we get him to help us find the guilty man?"

A dark scowl passed over the man's face. "Abe, you've been around the barn a few times. Don't ya know what he's doin'? 'Course he ain't gonna say he done it when there's redskin lovers around. Let him out to help us find the one who done it, he'll be gone, just like that."

Abe forced the man to meet his gaze. "Martha's right, then. You don't know who did it."

The man insisted the boy turned up with the exact number of nuggets immediately after the attack and robbery.

"How many people were on the Street at that same hour, do you suppose, had three nuggets? Did you check them all out? Turn him loose now."

Before the man figured out an answer, Martha rushed down the dark hall to the cell. "I couldn't find Gray Wolf or the others," she puffed. "But let's go talk to him." She approached the cell again.

The boy came as close as he could. He said something and a moment later Martha understood enough to realize he'd asked if he could go home. She turned to Abe. "He wants to go home."

Abe turned to the marshall. "Better set him loose, 'fore the US Government finds out you're holdin' an Indian without cause."

The man looked angry for a second, then shrugged. He pulled a long key chain from his pocket, unlocked the cage door, jerked the boy from the cell, and shoved him down the hall. The boy took off running and disappeared out the front door.

The jailer looked at Abe. "See? He done just what I said."

Abe hurried to the door and looked both ways. Then he saw the boy halfway down the block, still running. He stepped outside and gave a long loud whistle. The boy looked over his shoulder and kept going. "Hey! You! Wait up!" Abe motioned for the boy to come back. He didn't wait to see what the boy would do but ran toward him as fast as he could. And the boy waited! Abe could hardly believe his eyes. What would he do when he got there? He couldn't talk to the boy. A few moments later he reached the boy and stopped beside him. He held his hand out as if to shake hands but the boy didn't reciprocate. Then Abe heard Martha puffing up beside them.

The boy looked at her and smiled broadly. He said a whole paragraph of something. A moment later, Martha turned radiant eyes to Abe. "His name's Little Rain, and he can help us find the man who hurt and robbed the man."

Abe felt so excited he could hardly talk. "How's he going to do that?"

Martha said something to the boy but he only shook his head. "He doesn't understand me," she told Abe.

The boy said something else to Martha, pointed east down the Street, and started walking briskly. "He's taking us to the man who did the robbery," Martha told Abe as they followed him.

When they reached the building of the gold expert, the boy led them inside and pointed at the man who stood at the rough wood counter talking to a young couple.

Martha looked shocked. "He's saying Joseph Winieke did it," she said. "Do you believe it, Abe?"

Abe pointed at the man while looking at the boy. The boy nodded and motioned for Abe to go to the man. Abe moved over a bit and waited for the couple to finish and leave.

The couple didn't leave but the gold expert looked up. "C'n I help you folks? I'm jest talkin' to these people."

Abe put his hand on the boy's back and urged him to the counter. Martha followed. "Do you know this boy?" Abe asked Joseph Winieke.

The man looked at the Indian boy a moment. "Can't be sure. Might. Most everyone comes in here sooner or later. Hey! Ain't you the one brought in a big bag of nuggets?"

"Yes, but this isn't about that. The law picked up this boy for beating up and robbing a man of three nuggets this morning. The boy says you did it."

The man didn't bat an eyelash. "Yeah, I did it. Hope that's

the last time too. Third time he walked off with my nuggets. If he does it a hunnerd times I'll get 'em back a hunnerd times. Might get rough one of these days too. A feller gets kinda tired of everthin' he has gettin' stoled."

Martha gave a little cry and hugged the boy tight. The boy said something and she nodded. Then she pointed at Joseph Winieke. "The man took it from him," she told the boy speaking clearly. "He just got it back."

The boy said something else and Martha nodded, then gave him a little push, smiling tenderly.

Abe watched, thinking what a fine mother she'd make one day soon. He took Martha's hand. "Let's go back to that officer and tell him what happened."

The man hardly commented when they told him what had happened. "Maybe you should ought to find the man who got beat and make him an example," Abe said as they walked out the door.

They walked over to where they were building Nate and Cynthia Butler's home and blacksmith shop. "See?" Abe said, proudly showing Martha. "Coming right along. I guess they'll be moving into the house in a week. Said they want me to build 'em some furniture."

He steered Martha toward their place. "Guess I could make us a good living now making furniture with all the new people in town. Hard to know whether to try farmin' and buildin' furniture both or to spend all my time on one 'er the other."

"You should do whatever you purely enjoy the most," Martha said.

They approached their place, which Abe knew would be full of people. He grinned and returned to the subject. "Trouble is I don't know which I like best. I enjoy most everything I do, my little Martha."

Josie met them before they reached the house, delighted

to see them. "I suppose you got too rambunctious and they threw you out of the house," Martha said, petting the big dog as they hurried on.

Melissa opened the door as Abe reached for it. "It must have been some big emergency," she said. "I have supper ready and everyone else is here. Hurry and get washed."

Abe told them what happened as they ate. "It's not the first time we've rescued the Indians from them," he said. "They don't seem to care who did it, just so they can catch someone, preferably not white."

Tom shook his light brown head. "They all forget the Indians were here first and we're the intruders, don't they?"

"Oh!" Martha's face looked animated. "I just remembered something purely important. That Indian boy is Cayuse and I don't understand much of their language. So I asked God to help me understand him—and He did! He really did. I didn't understand it all and it took me a bit to figure it out but I understood enough to get him out. He's with his family now, wherever they are. Thank You, Lord."

Abe grinned. "And the sheriff and marshall are disliking us more all the time."

Nate and Cynthia moved into their bare house a week later. The men spent another week building Nate's blacksmith shop, then started on Tom and Rachel's place. Melissa would live with Tom and Rachel for awhile at least.

Abe and his hired man milked the cows each morning, and Melissa helped Martha strain and give away many gallons of the milk. Abe hauled a lot to the general stores and saloons. The hay was ripening and looked good.

Abe joined the crew building Tom and Rachel's house each morning as soon as he could. Cleve and Riley worked every minute they could. Jackson worked most of each day, after arriving late, and was the only person working for wages. The Dorland house was going to be similar to the one they had in Oregon City, only larger. They used narrow boards, called clapboards, on the outside. The house looked colonial with two stories and large round pillars in the front.

About three weeks later, they'd nearly finished the roof. One day as the men shingled the steep roof, Jackson started to slide down. "Help!" he screamed. "I'm goin' down."

Riley dropped his hammer, ran the twenty feet to Jackson, and dove on top of him. Jackson nearly stopped, then both young men began to slide. Abe watched a moment in horror, then ran the thirty feet and threw himself on Jackson who was closer to the edge. Jackson stopped, but somehow Abe's jump flipped Riley around and he disappeared over the edge of the roof, eighteen feet above the ground.

Jackson struggled. "Lie still," Abe commanded looking around for something to anchor to. Cleve tossed Abe a rope and nailed the other end to the other side of the roof. Then he dropped his hammer and followed Tom down the ladder, barely touching the steps.

Abe maneuvered Jackson around. "Grab that rope," he said. Jackson did. "Now walk up the rope to the ridge, then to the end to the ladder." Jackson did as Abe told him and climbed down the ladder.

Abe couldn't wait to get on the ground before talking to God. "Lord, please, You gotta help Riley," he pleaded. "He's a real man, Lord, loves his wife and family, works hard, and he loves You too. Remember how he helped me build furniture for the church? Thanks, Lord. Thanks for caring for Riley."

Abe pulled himself to the ridge and down the ladder. Racing to the front of the house, he found Tom bending over Riley. Riley seemed very still.

"Do you know anything?" Abe whispered into Tom's ear.

"He's alive with a strong pulse and breathing well," Tom said. Then seeming to forget anyone was there he continued examining Riley.

Abe stood with his hands clenched into fists. "Thank You, Lord," he whispered quietly. "When we put ourselves in Your hands we know we'll be all right."

"Think you'd be able to help me, Abe?" Tom asked a moment later. "All I can find wrong is a broken leg and a big bump on the left side of his head."

Abe dropped to his knees beside Riley. "Just tell me what to do. I'm strong and steady."

Cleve stood watching the doctor work on his son. Watching his lips move slightly, Abe knew he was praying. Jackson seemed to have disappeared. Tom's eyes met Cleve's. "We're going to need some soft cloths and strong straight boards for splints. Could you get them, Cleve? Maybe at the general store?"

Cleve looked delighted. "I'll be back in a few minutes," he said over his shoulder as he hurried off.

Tom grinned. "I guess that's what you call doing two jobs at once. I thought it would be easier on him if he didn't watch us trying to get the bone back. Can you hold his body perfectly still while I work on his leg?"

Abe, on his knees, leaned over Riley and grabbed him under the arms and tightened his muscles. "I got him." As Abe looked up to see what Tom would do next he noticed a ring of people around them watching. He started to tell them to move on but held his tongue. Maybe at least part of the people were genuinely concerned. Besides it wouldn't do any good to tell them to leave. At least the people weren't making any noise, not even talking.

"All right," Tom said, "hang on—tight." Abe tightened his grip on Riley. Tom pulled and twisted until Abe could hardly keep Riley still. Tom rested a moment. He grinned at Abe. "Just as well Riley's sleeping through this, wouldn't you say?" Abe nodded but he also wished Riley would wake up. It just didn't seem right, him being unconscious like this.

Tom kept wrenching on Riley while Abe did his best to keep the young man from moving. After a time that seemed forever, Abe heard a popping sound, then Tom relaxed. "We did it, Pard. I never had a better helper. You must have iron muscles."

Abe grinned. "Been working purty hard for a long time. Guess that helps. Think Riley'll be all right now? I'd like to see him wake up purty soon." Abe looked up to see Cleve standing nearby, his arms full of things and a big smile across his face.

He handed the things to Tom. "It felt like McMorris took forever, but seems I made it just right."

Tom began wrapping the leg with the cloth. With Abe's help they soon had it well padded. Then the young doctor fastened the small but strong planed poles around the leg with twine Cleve had brought.

Tom jumped to his feet and Abe did the same. "Let's get him home," Tom said. "Where's that?"

"We'll take him to my place," Cleve said. "It's a little closer'n theirs. If he wants to go on we'll take him." He looked closely at his quiet son. "He's gonna be all right, ain't he, Doc?"

Tom nodded. "The swelling is receding already, but I want to stay with him until he's awake and doing better." He looked around. "Is there a carriage or something to take him to your place?"

Cleve snorted. "Not many carriages around this town. Most everyone uses wagons."

"I have a wagon down the street," an older man said from

the watching crowd. "It has springs and we can fix up a bed in a couple minutes."

Cleve nodded.

"Thanks," Tom said, "that'll be great."

Abe thanked God as he walked behind the wagon. *Life would be pretty scary without You,* he said silently. *You're mighty good to us puny little creatures.*

Twenty minutes later Tom, Cleve, and Abe laid Riley on a feather bed in Cleve and Mandy's cabin across the creek from Abe and Martha's place. "You go on with whatever you need to do," Tom said. "Mandy and I'll watch Riley. I expect him to come around anytime now. Certainly before supper."

Abe hurried across the creek to Martha. After her hug and kiss, Abe pushed her back. "Heard about Riley?" he asked.

"No!" She looked as if she might get hysterical but settled down. "Has something happened to him?"

Abe nodded and quickly went on. "Broke his leg, but he's goin' to be all right. Fell off Tom's roof awhile ago. We took him to Cleve and Mandy's just now." Should he tell her the rest?

Yes, Abe, the truth is always best.

"Hurt his head some too. Tom says it's better already and thinks he'll be wakin' up right away now."

Martha's eyes grew big, then she nodded. "If Tom says he's better, then he's better. What about Cleve and Jackson and Mr. Butler?"

"Nate's at home finishing up the last things on his shop. Jackson took off after Riley fell. Probably went home to Nellie. He almost fell too, Martha. Riley fell tryin' to save Jackson." How much should he tell Martha? If he didn't someone else would. "I tried to save them both and it almost seems I pushed Riley off while I grabbed Jackson."

He shook his head. "I sure feel bad about my part in it."

Martha hugged him close again. "You didn't do any such thing, Abe Noble. You're always saving someone, one way or another." She shoved him back. "How did I ever get so lucky, getting you? Oops! It wasn't luck. You are my most precious gift from God. After Jesus, of course. Thank You, God."

She led Abe into the house and fed him some vegetable soup with a big slice of soft homemade bread. "Are you going to be glad when we're alone again?" she asked.

He shook his head. "Well, I s'pose it'll be nice, but those babies are sure fun." A dark cloud tried to cover his personal little sky, but he chased it away. "I can tell how much we'll enjoy ours by watching them," he added to cheer them both up.

"Yes," she said quietly. "I purely want us to have a baby of our own."

Abe got up from the table. "Think we ought to go see if Jackson's all right?"

They were glad for the chance for a ride on the new horses with Willie and Speck. Since they weren't going far they let Josie run beside them. They found Jackson and Nellie taking a nap but all right. "Think you'll be able to come back to work tomorrow?" Abe asked Jackson. "Tom and Rachel are eager to get their house finished."

"I'm not letting him go up on that steep roof anymore," Nellie said. "He nearly fell too, you know."

"I know," Abe said. "Riley fell saving Jackson. I guess that makes him a hero."

Neither Nellie nor Jackson replied.

Later in the afternoon, Tom appeared at his new house where Abe and Cleve were putting on shingles. He climbed the ladder and sat on the ridge at the top. "You'll both be glad to know Riley's awake, seeing straight, and talking." He chuckled. "I wouldn't say he's very happy to be on his back for a month or two though."

Cleve laughed out loud—and when he laughed loud everyone nearby heard. "I guess he'll live through it. He better be thankful he's gonna get well. Coulda kilt him, you know."

Tom nodded. "It could have. But it didn't so let's just be thankful. Now, what can I do here?"

Abe put him to work and before the sun set they had one side of the roof shingled. Abe figured it would take two more days to finish the other side. The next day they found a young man eager to earn some money, so the four finished the roof.

During the following week they plastered the inside. Abe watched as they applied the whitish stuff to the inside of the walls. "Better not let Martha see this," he said. "When we built our house, there wasn't much to be had. It's a different world already."

After painting the plaster, they put hardwood floors down, sanded them smooth as glass, and rubbed oil into them until the boards shone. *What a house,* Abe thought. Maybe it was time for him and Martha to build a new one.

They finished Tom's house, then built a much smaller replica of it for his office. Then Tom and Rachel moved in. "I'm sure goin' to miss those babies," Abe said, as they carried in the few things that the Dorlands had hauled from Oregon City.

Rachel laughed. "You won't miss them, Abe. We're right here on your place so we'll be seeing you a lot."

Abe stopped in to see Riley nearly every day. Riley didn't take to his idle life well at all. Melissa read to him a lot and they played games, but Riley couldn't handle what he called wasting his time.

One day Abe noticed they hadn't seen Jackson and Nellie for awhile. "Why don't we ride over and see 'em tonight?" he asked Martha at supper. "A good ride would be fun for all of us and maybe we could take them a pie or gingerbread."

Martha hurried a gingerbread into the oven. As soon as she took it out she called Willie. "Can you go help Abe saddle the horses? We're going over to see Jackson and Nellie. We're taking a gingerbread and cream to eat too."

The last part got Willie into the mood. Almost as soon as Martha had poured some cream into a quart bottle, the horses stamped and nickered at the door.

"Race you!" Willie called as they rode toward the back of their place. He nudged Speck into a gallop before Abe and Martha had time to register his challenge.

"Come on, Ebb," Abe murmured leaning over the shiny black mane. "You going to take that?" The big horse leaned forward and burst into a moderate canter. Even in the relaxed pace he gained on Willie and Speck. Abe slowed him just a bit. "We don't want to ruin their fun," he told Ebb. "Just a little behind is just right."

Martha and Thunder tore up beside Abe and passed. Ebb voluntarily sped up until he ran beside Thunder. Abe signaled to Martha to wait. "Let Speck and Willie win," he said. "How'd you feel if you always lost to the big people?"

Before any of them wanted to quit, they reached Jackson and Nellie's cabin, which looked more like a shack. They'd never planted grass and Jackson had scattered junk all around the cabin. Abe shook his head. Least a man could do was keep his place tidy.

When they knocked on the door no one answered. Abe knocked again. Sounded like he heard some kind of sound inside. Could something be wrong? He pulled the latch to see if the door was locked. It opened. Though dark inside,

Abe saw Nellie lying on the settle. "Hello, Nellie," he called. "Can we come in?"

She looked up, then back down but didn't answer. "You better go see what's wrong," he whispered to Martha. "Willie and I'll wait here."

Martha went in. "Goodness, Nellie, it's dark in here." She pulled open the curtains and fastened them. "Is something wrong, Nellie?" she asked when she finished. Nellie didn't answer. "Are you sick?" Martha finally asked.

Nellie shook her head no, then handed Martha a piece of paper. Martha read it. "Abe, you better come in here," Martha said.

Abe stepped through the door and Martha handed him the letter. He read:

> *Dear Nellie,*
>
> *It ain't that I don't love you 'cause I do. But I'm thinkin' I'm not cut out for family life. When you find this I'll be a long way toward the east coast. I'm aimin' to get into the Union Army and clear out all them slaves. I won't worry about you 'cause Abe and Martha will take care of you. Good-bye. Wish me good luck in the military.*
>
> *Jackson Lawford*

nine

Martha felt faint. Jackson had run off and left Nellie! And her expecting. How could any man do that? Then she remembered how he'd run off and left her and Willie when their parents had died. What was the matter with her brother anyway?

"When did you find this note, Nellie?" she asked.

"Yester—" Nellie swallowed a hiccup. "Yesterday mornin' when I got up."

"Did he go to bed with you the night before?" Abe asked.

Nellie nodded and burst into tears. "He—he was so loving. I can't believe he did this." She threw herself into Martha's arms. "Martha, could someone have taken him and made him write that note?"

Martha looked over Nellie's shoulder at Abe. He shook his head. She pulled Nellie closer. "Gather up your things, Nellie. We're taking you home with us." Suddenly Martha had a positively horrible thought. "Nellie! Did Jackson take the nuggets we gave you?"

Nellie shrugged. "I can't find them." She burst into tears again. Martha looked at Abe, shook her head, and waited until Nellie calmed. "I think he did," Nellie finally said. "I think he took the nuggets. Every one of them."

Abe put his hand on Nellie's back. "Don't worry about the nuggets, Nellie. We have some more we can give you if Jackson doesn't come back."

"He won't come back. I been waiting all yesterday and all today. He won't come back. I'll never see him again."

90

Another rush of sobs shook her round body.

When Nellie quieted, Martha helped her gather her things. Then she went out after Nellie's horse. But it was gone too. Abe looked shaken. "Do you think something else could have happened to Jackson?" he asked softly

Martha shook her head. "The first thing I remembered was how horrible I felt when he left Willie and me on the Trail when Mama and Papa died. Being without him was awful, but the worst part was knowing he hadn't cared enough to help Willie and me when we needed him so desperately. I didn't know how to handle the oxen or anything. And I felt as bad about losing our parents as he did. It was purely awful, Abe."

Oh thank You, God, for my wonderful Abe. And bless Nellie. She needs Your love and assurance badly right now. Thank You, Father.

"I'm sure he left her, Abe. He's too lazy and weak to be responsible." They returned to the house to get Nellie.

Nellie struggled with a large bundle. "I forgot to tell you my horse is gone," she said.

"It's all right," Martha said. "You can ride with me on Thunder. I don't like to ride double but we're both small and we'll walk him. He's big and it isn't far."

"I can walk," Nellie whimpered.

Abe had walked up behind her. "You get on that horse, Nellie. I'll help you up." He helped her up, then hurried to Ebb carrying Nellie's big bag.

"Race you!" Willie screamed touching Speck's sides with his heels. Martha smiled as the two raced off ahead. "Are you all right back there, Nellie?" she asked.

Nellie didn't answer, but Martha felt Nellie's chin bump her back as she nodded her head. Thunder didn't like plodding home so far behind the other horses. Every little while he pranced and turned nervously.

"He doesn't like me on here," Nellie said after Martha had soothed and quieted him a few times. "Let me walk, Martha. It isn't far."

Martha's tinkly laugh rang in the air. "He doesn't mind you at all, Nellie. What he hates is me holding him back. He knows he could beat the other two even with both of us on him." She giggled, "But it's good for him to be humbled a little."

When they reached the house, Abe had already put Nellie's things into Willie's room—the room Abe had slept in when they first married.

"Willie can sleep in our room for now," Abe said softly to Martha.

"Please, can he sleep with me?" Nellie whined. "I hate being alone."

Abe looked at Martha and she shook her head. "Ask him," she mouthed.

He grinned. "We'll see, Nellie. If he thinks it would be good fun to sleep with you he probably will."

Martha could tell Abe worked extra hard to keep everyone laughing at supper that evening. Willie took it up and even Nellie laughed a few times.

Nellie also ate a big meal. "I didn't eat anything after Jackson left," she said. "At first I kept waiting for him to come back so we could eat together, then I couldn't seem to get hungry."

Nellie put on a brave front, helping Martha and playing with Willie all evening. When they finished worship and Nellie invited him to share her bedroom, he willingly went.

After Abe kissed Martha goodnight, she couldn't fall asleep but lay very still. The house creaked. Two men far away yelled, and several dogs barked. Josie, on a rug at the foot of their bed, didn't make a sound.

Suddenly Abe leaned on his elbow. "Have you noticed how nice Tom and Rachel's house is?" he whispered.

Martha burst out laughing. "How did you know I'm awake?"

He put an arm around her and pulled her close, her back to his chest. "With all that sighing, how I could I not know? Well, have you noticed?"

She turned to face him in the dark. "Yes. It's going to be just right for a doctor and his family."

"But would you like a new house—something like theirs?"

"Abe! Why would we need a fine house like that?"

He chuckled. "Seems we already need an extra bedroom—for Willie. And no tellin' how long Nellie'll be with us. In a year or two her babe'll be needin' a room."

Long silence.

"Well, I think you deserve a nice house, Martha. You've done without long enough."

Martha couldn't believe her ears. But she should have known. Abe would do anything for her. That was just how he was. "I don't know, Abe. Let's sleep on it. If you still think it's a good idea, we'll ask God in the morning. I purely don't want anything in the whole world if He doesn't think it's best."

"Right. Are you sleepy now?"

The next morning Nellie slept until after the animals were cared for, the milk given away and sold, breakfast was ready, and Martha awakened her.

"Can I help you?" Nellie asked.

Martha hadn't been sure Nellie would ask but she'd given it some thought. Nellie would be happier keeping busy. Besides she really could help. She smiled at her pudgy sister-in-law. "Of course you can, Nellie. Would you rather cook? Or clean and wash clothes? That's most of the indoor work. I won't ask you to work outside."

"I can't cook much," Nellie said. "Jackson didn't care whether I cooked or not. We usually ate meat sandwiches. I can clean and wash clothes though. I bet I can do that nearly as good as you, Martha."

Jackson didn't have any right to expect Nellie to do anything, Martha thought. He hardly worked. "I was hoping you'd say that," she said out loud. "I love cooking and baking. I can do that and have more time to do my outside work too." She hugged Nellie. "Oh Nellie, I'm so sorry my brother is such a cad, but I'm excited to have you here. It's going to be fun."

"I don't know what's going to be fun about it, but we'll be all right," Nellie sniffed. Then her eyes brightened. "Remember when you lived in your wagon at the end of the Street and we waded in the creek—and fell down?"

Martha remembered. "You didn't care a bit. You just danced around until you dried, then went home to help your ma as if nothing happened."

Nellie looked pensive. Martha thought she might burst into tears. "How was it, living with Jackson?" Martha asked. "Was he kind and thoughtful? Or a selfish pig like he's acting now? This is just what he did when our parents died on the Trail, you know. He went off and left me to care for Willie and also the oxen and everything."

Nellie smiled. "He treated me like his own queen, Martha. Really he did. That's why I'm so surprised—and why it's so hard."

Martha nodded, happy that at least Jackson was a good enough man to treat his wife well.

That night, when they finally found themselves alone, Abe asked her again if she'd like to have a house like Rachel's.

Martha giggled. "I don't know what I'd do with a fine house like that," she said. "Isn't this one good enough, Abe?"

He grinned. "Well, seems to be gettin' smaller all the time. Tom and Rachel just moved into their own house. Now Nellie's here. Soon her little babe will be too. We're goin' to be crowded."

"Could we build another room? Or even two?"

Abe shook his head. "You're just a simple girl, aren't you? Maybe that's part of why I love you so much. But you'd love a nice house, Martha, after you lived in it awhile."

"Maybe we better ask God what He wants us to do, Abe. If He wants us to have a bigger and better house, I'll go along with it." She giggled. "If we do build a fine new house I want a room in it that even Rachel doesn't have."

He looked surprised. "What room would that be?"

"A bathroom, Abe. I read in *The Statesman* that everyone's building bathrooms in their houses back East."

"What's a bathroom?"

"Abe! Just what it says. A nice room with a tub and towels and everything you need to take a bath. Think how nice it would be to take a bath anytime you want, no matter who's in the kitchen. I think that would be purely heaven, Abe. You'd never believe how fancy the bathrooms are in some places. In some of them you just pull a plug and the water runs out the bottom of the tub. And—"

Abe looked as if he'd seen a bright light. "Yeah!" he interrupted. "You're right, as usual, my little Martha. I say we build a house with a bathroom."

She shook her head. "Not until we talk to God about it."

So they knelt, held hands, and asked God to guide them in every little thing, and especially right now to let them know if they should build a house.

"All right," Abe said when they finished. "Let's both be

listenin'." He tweaked her ear. "I got a little pushy, I know, but I really want to do what my Pard up there wants."

Martha listened—as she set bread; as she put a roast surrounded by potatoes, carrots, and onions into the oven; and as she picked bugs from the potato plants and put them in a tall jar with a small neck. When she finished, she would pour boiling water into the jar. She had to do this every week. If she didn't they'd lay eggs on the underside of the potato leaves. When the larvae hatched, they would make short work of the potato plants. Seemed like every kind of bug thrived here. Even more so than in Missouri. She smiled to herself. She really didn't blame the bugs for settling in Walla Walla. They couldn't choose a nicer place to live.

After she finished with the bugs, she hoed the potatoes, still listening for God. *Well, He'd speak to Abe. He always spoke to Abe.* As she worked, waited, and thought, she began to get excited about the house. How wonderful to be able to take a bath without chasing everyone out of the house.

At dinner, Nellie and Willie teased each other, seeming to have great fun. Nellie had the washing hanging on the line and the house looked neat. Abe and Martha talked quietly together, comparing what they'd accomplished that morning.

When they finished eating, Martha started to wash the dishes. "That's my job," Nellie said. "It's cleaning, isn't it?"

"No, it's finishing the cooking," Martha explained. The girls ended up doing the dishes together.

As Martha hurried out to feed the cows, Abe met her. "Hear anything from upstairs?" he asked.

She shook her head. "No. I thought for sure you would."

He helped her wash windows during the afternoon. "How's Nellie doing?" he asked while they mixed vinegar and water to make more window cleaner.

Martha straightened up and rubbed her lower back. "Better than I expected. I thought she might not know how to do anything in the house. She's trying to be cheerful, too. It must be hard, expecting a baby without a man to help."

As they talked Nellie approached. "Martha," she called, "I can't find anything more to do in the house. Can I help you out here?"

Abe handed her his washing rags and headed for the barns.

"Do you know how to do this?" Martha asked, "or do I need to show you?"

Nellie grinned. "Just show me which windows need cleaned. I'll get them clean one way or another."

As the sun sank toward the west, Martha knew she'd better get supper going for her family. "Come on, Nellie," she invited. "You've done well today and must be tired." Josie, who had been lying in the soft warm earth, followed them into the house.

Later that night, after Nellie and Willie had gone to bed, Martha and Abe sat across the table talking as they drank coffee. "Still didn't hear anything?" he asked.

She shook her head, hardly believing he hadn't either. "Do you think He'll want us to build?" she asked.

Abe nodded. "Sure. Why would He care? I don't mind tellin' you I like your bathroom idea a whole lot. Why didn't I think of that a long time ago?"

Martha felt relieved. "I'm getting purely excited about it too. A big house with lots of room for everyone and everything would be real nice." She giggled. "Who knows? We may have half a dozen babies a few years from now. Might as well get ready for them, don't you think?"

Abe jumped from his chair, ran around the table, and pulled her close. "Thank you, Martha my own," he whispered.

"This is the first time you said right out that you want a lot of children. I do too."

Her heart felt as if it would beat right through her chest. She turned her face up to his kiss. Ummmm. How she loved him! How could it possibly have taken so long for her to find out. "Yes, I want lots of children, Abe. And I'm ready right now."

They finished their coffee and oatmeal cookies, and went to bed, arm in arm.

The next morning everyone did what they had to do to get the day going: milk the cows, give and sell the milk, make breakfast, and whatever. When they finished and before they went to the fields, Abe invited Martha to go buy groceries with him. As they passed the new Dorland home and medical office Abe suggested they stop a minute to see how the family was getting along.

After Rachel squealed her pleasure and invited them in, Martha looked at everything with new eyes. She would no doubt soon have a house similar to this one. Except hers would have a bathroom. The large living room, painted a soft green, looked inviting with colorful area rugs covering the hardwood floors.

"Come into the kitchen," Rachel said, "and we'll have a cup of coffee while we talk. Tom's in his office. He's had a couple of patients already. Oh, Martha, we're so glad we've come here."

As they talked, two horses thundered up to the house, stopping so quickly dirt flew from under their hooves. The riders jumped down and beat on the door.

"Where's the doc?" one of the whiskered men asked. "We're with the wagon train that's comin'. It'll be in town in a few days, maybe tomorrow. Thing is, we left two wagons in the Blue Mountains. An axle broke on one and the other'n turned over comin' down the steep grade. Broke all to pieces and fell on one of the men helpin'. Pro'ly broke a leg. Had to leave 'im up there. His wife stayed to care for 'im."

The other man broke in. "Couple doctors in town told us you're new here and probly don't have nuthing to do. Could the doc come back with us?"

Rachel called Tom and explained what had happened. He grinned and held his hand out to first one of the men, then the other. "I have a few patients, boys, maybe five. But they aren't very sick. I think I can go." He turned to Abe. Could you go get Rachel's father?" He turned to the men. "He's a blacksmith and may be able to get the wagon fixed."

Abe and Martha hurried to the Street, to Nate's shop that they had built on the lot they'd sold to him. He said he would be ready to go in a half hour. Cynthia asked Martha to tell Rachel she would come down and stay with her while the men were gone and help her. She giggled when she said it, so Martha knew she needed Rachel.

As they walked back, Abe seemed quiet. "What's wrong? Are you worried about that trip into the Blues?"

Abe grinned. "Not exactly. But I thought maybe I'd go and help."

ten

As Abe hurried getting things ready, he wished they'd had an answer about the house. Never mind. When God wanted them to know, they'd know.

Tom banged on the door and came in. "I need a horse, Abe, and so does Nate. Where can we get some in a hurry?"

Abe let them ride Thunder and Ebb to Fort Walla Walla. They soon found horses they liked and rode them back home, leading Abe and Martha's horses. The men from the wagon train said they'd buy supplies while the others got horses. They showed up about the same time Abe, Tom, and Nate did.

"How long do you think it'll take us to get there?" Abe asked Wally, the younger of the men.

"It's about eighty miles. We left there day before yesterday. Rode purty hard. Stopped and rested about four or five hours each night. Ate bread as we rode."

"Ebb's a good mover," Abe said, "but when he's tired I rest him no matter what."

Tom nodded. "Me too. I haven't had Thor long but I don't intend to override him, either. That all right, boys?"

The taller one, Irv, said it was all right but they needed to make as good time as they could.

When Abe kissed Martha good-bye he wished he hadn't decided to go. No, he couldn't wish that. Someone needed him. The five riders took off south at a gentle canter. Starting out like this reminded Abe of the gold hunting expedition. An important element was missing from this group. Martha. He leaned forward and petted Ebb's shiny black neck. "We'll just make the trip as quick as possible, won't we?" he asked the huge horse.

They stopped several hours after dark, watered the horses, then let them graze. The men ate meat sandwiches Martha had made. "Better enjoy this meal," Tom said. "I think all we have after this is bread and dried apples.

When Abe dropped onto his blanket, he turned his eyes toward the starry sky. So starry he couldn't separate the stars. "You up there, Lord?" he asked. "I hope You agree with what we're doin'."

You're doing what's right, Abe.

Abe wanted to talk to Him some more. Abe knew he had something to talk about, but he fell asleep trying to remember.

Darkness still hid the world when Irv shook him awake. "Wally says we gotta go," he said loudly. "Them people in the mountains may need us right bad."

The other man, Wally, woke Tom and Nate. The men grabbed some dry bread and ate it as they hurried toward the Blues. The horses all seemed eager to go, even though the sun hadn't risen yet. "It's cause it's cool," Irv said. "Horses don't much like hot weather. Neither do I."

They made good time most of that day, stopping late at night again, this time in the Blue Mountains. About mid-morning the next day they reached the wagon with the broken axle and the injured man. A young woman ran to meet them. "I'm so glad you got here," she said. "Ray's sicker. Now he doesn't even know what happened or where he is."

Tom leapt off Thor before she finished talking. "Where is he?" Tom asked quietly.

"Over here," the woman said, leading the way to the wagon. As Abe watched the two, his admiration for Tom grew. If something ever happened to him—*Please no, Lord*—he'd sure like Tom to be nearby.

The man lay on a folded blanket on the ground behind the disabled wagon. Tom dropped to his knees beside him. "Hello, Ray. I'm Tom Dorland and I've come to help you. I'm a doctor. Where are you hurt?"

The man looked at Tom as though seeing through a deep fog. "You a doc?" He sighed loudly. "Good." He relaxed and closed his eyes.

"Hurt pretty bad?" Tom asked. The man nodded without opening his eyes. Tom didn't force the man to try to talk anymore but began going over his arms, legs, and body. After several minutes of examining and reexamining, he turned back to the woman. "The men were right. He has a broken leg. His right arm's also broken. How long's it been since this happened?"

The woman thought a moment and shook her head. "I'm not sure. Four, five days—maybe a week." Her lips turned up in a tiny smile. "It's been a long, long time."

Nate, Irv, and Wally turned away from Ray and began working on the wagon.

Tom leaned back over the man, running his fingers over the right leg and arm. Then he met Abe's eyes. "I'm not sure we can set them now. Depends how much they've healed." He shook his head. "Sure would have been easier when it first happened."

"Let's get it over," Abe said. "We both know what we gotta do." He grinned at Tom. "Remember, I'm experienced at this stuff now. Ready for me to hold him?"

Tom shook his head. "Not yet. I have a tiny bit of something new in my bag, and I doubt we'll ever need it more."

He pulled out a tiny bottle, unscrewed the top, took a small cloth, and poured a few drops on it. "I have something here for you to smell, Ray," he said softly to the man. "It won't smell too good but it'll help the pain a whole lot. Do you understand?"

Ray nodded and reached for the cloth. Tom didn't release it to him but looked to the woman. "Could you hold this over his nose until I tell you to stop?"

She quickly took the cloth and did as Tom asked.

When Ray relaxed, Tom nodded. "Hold him, Abe. This isn't going to be easy. I'll start on the arm—it'll probably go better than the leg."

Abe held with all his strength as Tom pushed, pulled, and twisted. The man didn't seem to feel anything. After a few minutes Tom told the woman to take the cloth away. "When he starts hurting, put it back," he instructed. The woman nodded.

Abe thought the ordeal would go on forever, with Tom repeating the hard thrusts and twists. Finally when Abe thought he couldn't hold the man any longer he heard a loud pop.

"There," Tom said with a relieved sigh. "It just rebroke. Now it'll set easily." Only a few minutes later another small snap told Abe the bone had slipped into place.

"Can I let go now?" he asked, lifting his eyes to Tom's.

Abe could hardly believe his eyes. Sweat covered Tom's entire face. He looked red and tired, and breathed hard. He dropped to the ground. "Yeah, let go. Next thing we gotta do is wrap it." He retrieved the three lighter wooden dowels he'd brought and the lengths of soft material. After wrapping the arm and securing it firmly, he turned to Abe. "How was that for a day's work?"

"Tough," Abe said. "Harder for you than me, though." He glanced at the man whose eyes rested on Tom. "Probably hardest of all on Ray."

"I'm going to let Ray rest awhile before we set his leg," Tom said. He glanced at the woman. "Don't want to push too much chloroform at him too fast. I guess he hasn't eaten for awhile. The chloroform upsets the stomach sometimes if it's full."

Abe walked over to the men at the wagon. "How you doin'?" he asked. "Think you'll have it fixed today?"

Nate grinned but shook his head. "We're workin' as fast as we can, Abe, but this is slow, hard work. Maybe tomorrow afternoon."

Abe returned to Tom and his patient. Tom asked the man, Ray, how he got hurt. "Helpin' a wagon down a steep hill. Thing turned over on me. Hurt oxen—had to shoot 'em." He attempted a chuckle. "Lucky they didn't shoot me too."

"Well, you're lucky," Tom said. "We won't have to shoot you this time. You're going to be just fine. Are you ready to do the leg now?"

The man nodded. "Be glad when it's over."

Tom poured a bit more chloroform into the cloth and handed it to the woman. After doing a few more preparations and bowing his head a moment, Tom tensed up. "All right, use the chloroform. Be sure to take it away when he relaxes and use it again when he feels pain. Abe, hold him absolutely still." After five minutes Abe decided Tom wasn't going to be able to rebreak the leg.

"Think we oughta get one of those boys to hold him so I could help you?" Abe asked.

Tom didn't answer but shook his head. Abe still held the

man in a grip of iron. After a bit Ray began moving and moaning. "Give him the cloth," Tom commanded. A moment later the man quieted. Then Abe heard a loud snap and "Thank You, Lord," in a quiet whisper. "All right, Abe, hold him while I put the bone together." A few minutes later a much smaller pop was followed by a huge sigh from Tom.

"It's all over," he said. "Thank You, God. I could never have done it without You." He turned to the woman. "Take away the cloth."

Tom and Abe sat on a low log for a few minutes. The woman sat on another one nearby. "You fellows hungry?" she asked. "Before the train left, they cut a back leg off one of the oxen and I've been frying slices of that. I have flour and things to make trail bread too."

Tom nodded. "Thanks—uh, you know we never have gotten your name."

"I'm Ray's wife, Sandra. Call me, Sandy."

Tom smiled. "Thanks for your good help, Sandy. We couldn't have done it without you. We still have to finish with Ray, then I'll bet everyone would like some of that meat." He smiled. "I feel as though I've done a big day's work. How about you, Abe?"

Abe nodded. He didn't feel as hungry as he did tired at the moment, but he knew he'd soon be hungry enough.

The woman put her hand on Tom's arm. "I can't thank you enough, Doctor. Do you think my husband will be all right now?"

"As right as rain, Sandy. It'll take a while to heal but after that, he won't even limp. Come on, Abe. Let's finish fixing that leg."

Sure enough after they finished the leg, Abe felt ravenous and hardly able to wait until Sandy had everything fixed.

Tom told her to boil a piece of meat until it fell apart and feed Ray the meat with the juice.

The men fixing the wagon washed up in the nearby creek with Tom and Abe.

"Comin' along all right," Nate volunteered after they had prayed and filled the tin pans Sandy had provided. "We should have it ready to roll by noon tomorrow."

"Will Ray be ready to go by then?" Abe asked Tom.

"I think so." Tom turned to Sandy. "Can we haul him in the wagon? It'll be bumpy but he'll be all right."

She nodded. "Yes. They took our wagon on and left us only the one with the broken axle so we won't have so many wagons to worry with when we get going. But there are plenty of blankets in this one to make him a bed."

By noon the next day Ray was much better and eager to go on. Sandy had fed him beef broth and well-boiled meat almost continually since Tom had told her to.

Nate and the men put the finishing touches on the wagon about three o'clock in the afternoon. "May as well start," Abe said. "Nothing here to keep us until mornin'—or even one hour longer."

Everyone agreed so Sandy put all but one blanket under Ray and the men lifted him in as gently as possible. They gathered the horses and oxen and started the slow procession home.

"Don't worry," Ray said. "Don't hurt nuthin' like it did before Doc fixed it."

They traveled for several hours, before stopping to eat sandwiches Sandy had made from her meat and Abe's bread. Ray ate a sandwich with the rest of them. "I'm nigh well already, Doc. Hardly feel a twinge, even ridin' in that wagon."

Tom gripped the man's shoulder. "You're doing great, Ray, but you aren't even started healing yet. You realize I had to rebreak both your arm and leg don't you?" Ray reluctantly admitted he knew.

They hadn't gone far when Abe heard some kind of ruckus in the bushes south of the trail. He listened, nudged Ebb toward the sound, until through the brushes he saw three doe deer, one fawn with barely visible spots, and two gray animals that looked like large dogs. Wolves! He would bet those animals were wolves, and no doubt trying to get the fawn.

He hurried Ebb back to the trail. "Come on," he called softly. "Somethin's goin' on over here I don't like much."

Nate, Tom, and Irv quickly joined Abe where they could see the animals. Suddenly Tom pointed. "Look!" he said. "The fawn's tangled in something and the wolves are going to get it."

"No they ain't," Nate yelled. "We're stoppin' those things."

"I'll get my gun," Irv said. "I'll fix them."

"You aren't goin' to shoot 'em," Abe said. "Martha would disown me."

"And Rachel would shoot me," Tom said. "Go ahead and get the gun anyway. Maybe we can scare them away."

"You'll scare the does away too," Nate said. "Then what'll the little one do?"

While they tried to decide what to do, the animals became aware of their presence. The wolves took off through the brush, the doe deer gracefully leapt over a few logs and out of sight too. The fawn struggled but didn't go anywhere.

"I'm goin' over there," Abe said. "You fellows watch for them wolves. You know they're watchin' us." He slid off Ebb's back and walked softly toward the fawn. It didn't move an eyelash. *It's hopin' I don't see it,* Abe thought.

"Lord, I'm tryin' to help Your little creature here. You help me do it without anyone or anything gettin' hurt, all right?"

You're doing fine, Abe.

When he reached the fawn, he saw it had thoroughly tangled itself in a kind of cord the Indians used for fishing. *Those buzzards,* Abe thought. *I'd a thought they'd know better.* As he examined the cord, he realized he could never untangle it from the terrified animal—even if it continued holding still.

He hurried back to the others. "It's Indian fishin' cord," he said, "and it's really tangled up. I ain't got a knife, either. I need a knife and someone to hold the fawn while I cut that stuff off."

Nate handed him a knife and Irv followed him to the fawn. "You wanta hold it or cut?" Abe asked. The man felt more secure holding than trying to cut off the tight cords.

Abe opened the knife. "You hold still, little one," he said softly. "We're trying to help you."

The fawn barely breathed while Abe pulled the cord loose from its body, stuck the knife in, and cut. He repeated the action innumerable times while the little animal held perfectly still. "We got to be careful not to let you get away when I got the cords only partway off," he murmured, cutting, pulling out, cutting. Finally the last loop fell to the ground. "You can go now," he said, lifting the fawn to its feet and giving it a little push. "Go find your mama, baby."

When the fawn discovered itself free, it took off like a big jack rabbit through the bushes. Abe smiled, closed the knife, and returned to the men. "Hope it finds its mama," he said.

Abe felt real good the rest of the day. They stopped hours

after dark, released the animals to graze, and threw down their blankets.

They started the next morning before sunrise and traveled hard all day. By the next day they had nothing to eat but Sandy's trail bread and side meat. No one refused the simple fare.

They arose before sunrise every day, ate dry bread on the trail and rode long days. The travel wasn't hard on either the people or the animals, not even the oxen, as the trail was good and mostly flat.

Ray grew better each day and his happy spirit encouraged everyone, especially Sandy. One day Abe asked him where his wagon train was headed.

"Oregon City," Ray said with a mischievous grin. "Sandy 'n I ain't, though. I ain't gettin' away from Doc for a long time. Or never."

"I've been in Oregon City," Tom said. "Take my word for it, Walla Walla's a better place to settle. Better medical care too."

Finally, Abe stood on a hill overlooking the Walla Walla Valley. A day later, they arrived home. After greeting Martha and Willie, Abe asked where Nellie was.

"She's doing poorly," Martha said. "I have her in bed." She looked concerned. "She's been having pains nearly all the time since you left. I'd like Tom to look at her."

"Too bad to interrupt his homecoming, but I'll go get him," Abe said, heading out the door.

"The Indians came for food and another Bible story. They're always eager to hear more. You heard anything from your Pard since you left?" Martha called.

"He was with us," Abe called back.

He returned with Tom a half hour later and went out to

check the livestock. Martha followed. "What did He say?" she asked.

"Nothing. He just came along with me. He's always glad to help someone."

"No, Abe. I don't mean Tom. I mean your Pard."

Oh, she meant the Lord. "I don't remember exactly, Martha. He just let me know He was with us."

"Abe! Don't you remember what you were going to ask Him?"

Abe thought. And thought. Finally it popped into his head. The house! Did God want them to build a new house? He laughed. "I plumb forgot all about that big problem, Martha. Didn't think about it once while we traveled."

eleven

Martha couldn't believe her ears! They'd thought of little else for the last few days before he left. How could he possibly forget all about it? "Abram Noble, I don't think you even want a new house!"

He grinned again. "I do if the Lord wants us to, Martha. You taught me to feel that way. But we were purty busy up there in the mountains. First we fixed the man and the wagon which kept all our thinkin' real busy. Then we had to go slow since we had a wagon and a hurt man." Then he remembered the deer and the wolves, so he told her about that.

"Abe, you're the world's best man. No one else would have taken the time to help a little animal."

Abe held her tight for a moment, then released her so he could look into her beautiful gray eyes. "You're wrong, Martha. Everyone wanted to help the deer. Tom said Rachel would scalp him if he didn't help."

Oh yes, Martha remembered how much Rachel loved animals. Almost a passion. She nodded. "True, Abe. Rachel purely loves animals. Maybe more than I do."

"Well, I just want you to know all of the men were in there fighting for the little fawn's life. What did Tom say when he saw Nellie?"

"I left, Abe. I wanted to know about the house. I've asked many times every day but haven't an inkling what He wants us to do."

Abe put his arm over her shoulders and steered her toward the house. "We'll know, Martha. He'll tell us what to do."

Soon after they reached the house, Tom appeared from Nellie's bedroom. "She's definitely having contractions. Better keep her in bed until they quit and for awhile after. The baby could never live. Not possible at six months." He pulled up a chair and plopped down astraddle, leaning his elbows across the back. "She says her husband left her. Do you think he'd come back to save the baby?"

Martha felt her heart lurch. "We think he went back East. He left a note saying he was going to join the military and free the slaves." She sniffed. "He doesn't like responsibility and may have gone because of the baby. He's a cad."

Tom sighed and got to his feet. "Do anything you can to make her happier. Maybe you can get her excited about the baby."

Martha went into Nellie's room. "You don't want to lose your baby, do you?" she asked kindly.

Nellie shook her head. "No, but how can I take care of a baby by myself?"

Martha sat on the bed beside Nellie and stroked her hair. "You're not by yourself. You know that, Nellie. We're here for you. Your ma's just down at the Street too."

"Ma told me Jackson wasn't any good, Martha. She'd never help me after I married him anyway."

"Well, we will. Don't worry about a thing." She thought of something that might cheer Nellie. "I'll tell you a secret," she whispered, though no one else could possibly hear. "We're thinking about building a new house. Not for sure, but we're thinking. If we do we'll be sure to make lots of room for you and the baby."

Nellie didn't look impressed.

"Look, Nellie," Martha said, "I've been wanting a baby so bad it hurts. But so far I'm not having one. Now, I'm thrilled about yours and can't wait to help you take care of it. What do you want, Nellie? A boy or a girl?"

Nellie stiffened just a little. Martha knew she was having another pain. "I'd love for you to have a beautiful, dainty little girl just like you," Martha said. "We can make gorgeous little frilly clothes for her. Won't that be fun?"

"How can I talk about clothes when I'm hurting so bad?" Nellie cried.

"You're right, Nellie. I'm sorry. I have a better idea. Let's ask God to stop the pains so you can enjoy waiting for your little girl."

Without waiting for Nellie's answer she dropped to her knees beside the bed. "Dear Father, we thank You for blessing us so much. We especially thank You for one of Your biggest blessings— Nellie's baby. It's not time for it to be born, Father." She giggled softly. "You knew that, didn't You? Father, we're asking You to stop her pains and help her baby grow big enough. We pray in Jesus' name and thank You so much for hearing and answering our prayers. Amen."

Martha got up. "Everything's all right now, Nellie. You won't have even one more pain. I just know you won't."

"Everything's not all right, Martha. Maybe it is for you, but it's not for me. Now I can't even work to earn my food. I'm not a bit sure I want this baby, Martha. And God doesn't want me to have it either."

Martha tinkled her sweet laugh. "God does want you to have it, Nellie. And you're going to, so why don't you start wanting it too?"

Nellie's next pain was lighter, the next one lighter yet—

and the pains ended.

That night after they thanked God for ending Nellie's pains, they asked Him to help them know whether they should build a new house or live in the old one. When they finished, Martha gave Abe instructions to listen carefully for God to answer.

"I will, little Martha," Abe said. "You listen too."

The next morning neither knew His will. "Let's not get impatient," Abe said. "As long as we don't hear, we know it isn't time to build a new house yet."

Martha kept Nellie in bed for several days after the pains quit, though Nellie insisted she should be helping. She let Nellie get up for the first time to go to church that weekend.

With Abe and Martha's generous gifts, the church had been enlarged to accommodate the more than a hundred regular attenders. Riley had helped Abe build the needed pews as he had done when the church first began. Abe always said the people who went to church probably weren't out rustling cattle or hurting their fellow men.

Martha started sewing for the baby in earnest and tried to get Nellie to help. Nellie stitched a few diapers but usually found something else to do.

After Nellie went a month without pains, Martha and Abe bought her a little sorrel mare. "Not for you to ride now," Martha said. "We just wanted you to have something to look forward to later."

When the hay ripened, Rachel helped Nellie and Martha prepare food for the harvesters. Nellie did her part willingly without complaint but never seemed to get over Jackson's leaving. And she had never heard from him or about him.

❧

About the first of December Nellie's pains started up again.

Tom came. "It's still a little early," he said after examining her, "but I think the baby will be all right. And I don't think we'll be able to stop the pains."

He guessed right. That night, about eighteen hours later, Nellie had a healthy little girl. Martha noticed she didn't get very excited about the baby, but then she'd had a hard afternoon and evening.

Martha couldn't contain her excitement. "Look, Abe," she said, pulling the little quilt back so he could see the tiny face and fists waving aimlessly. "Isn't that the most perfect little thing you ever saw?"

Abe's face expressed the awe Martha felt in the presence of God's little miracle of life. "Know what I want even worse than a house?" he whispered.

Martha nodded. "I purely do too, Abe. I do. Maybe soon."

Nellie nursed her baby but didn't take much interest in its care. Martha brought her to Nellie often and always bathed the baby in Nellie's room so she could watch.

"See how clear her eyes are getting?" Martha asked one day. "She may be able to see your face now, Nellie. Smile at her so she knows how much you love her."

Although a week had passed since the baby's birth, Nellie hadn't offered to get out of bed. Neither had she named the baby. One afternoon when Martha finished her work early, she plopped down on Nellie's bed. "Let's think of the prettiest names we know. This perfect baby has to have the most beautiful name in the whole world."

"I don't know any pretty names."

"Nellie! You do too. How do you like Elizabeth? You could call her Beth or Lizzie or Betty. Or how about Susan? Susie. Or Kathleen? That's extra pretty."

"Do we really have to do this right now, Martha? I'm tired."

Martha gave up and prepared supper. What could she do to make Nellie feel better? She would feel awful if Abe left her and she had a baby alone. She knew she would, so she couldn't blame Nellie.

Melissa, Riley's wife, came to sit with Nellie often. Martha didn't have time to stay while they visited but it looked to her is if Nellie didn't welcome their old friend very much.

Martha talked to Tom. "She's doing fine physically," he said, "but she seems to have lost interest in any and everything. I thought the baby would cheer her up but so far it hasn't."

"Maybe she needs to get to work," Martha suggested.

Tom nodded. "An interest in something would be fine. But she feels she and the baby are a huge imposition on you and Abe. I'm afraid she'd take it wrong if you tried to involve her in the work."

Martha tried to excite Nellie about buying Christmas presents for Babykins, as Martha had started calling the nameless baby. Nellie performed her responsibilities like a trained animal, doing well whatever she attempted, but without enthusiasm. She took no interest at all in spending Martha and Abe's money for Christmas presents or anything else.

Abe made the baby a beautiful cradle for Christmas and Martha made her a soft blanket, frilly dress, and heavy matching coat. They gave Nellie a nice church dress and heavy coat. Nellie didn't even try them on and barely thanked them for the gifts.

Martha finally became indignant. "Even if I could get Jackson to come back I wouldn't!" she said to Abe. "He doesn't deserve this beautiful family after the way he's broken Nellie's heart. And if it weren't for us, that baby wouldn't know what love is."

The winter progressed with some snow and cold weather but nothing unbearable. Still they didn't have an answer about the new house.

Abe made furniture and had more orders than he could fill. "I could make us a good livin' doin' this," he said. "But it's so much fun gettin' outside in the spring and helpin' God start things growin'."

Martha loved him so much and felt terribly proud of him. "Why don't you keep on making furniture in the winter and farming in the summer?"

He nodded. "I guess I'll do that for now at least. One of these days a good furniture maker will show up and I'll be finished."

"No you won't, Abe Noble. No one's going to beat your furniture."

One day in February the sun came out and shone like a warm spring day. Abe and Willie invited Martha to go riding with them. "Nellie," Martha called. "Come go for our first spring ride. I'll carry Babykins so you'll be free to ride on the wings of the wind. Did you know God does that? Rides on the wings of the wind? In His chariot, a cloud." Nellie didn't know—nor did she want to go riding. They locked Josie in the house with Nellie.

"Where shall we go?" Willie asked as they rode out of the corral and Abe shut the gate. "I want to go a long long ways."

Abe appeared to give it much thought. "We could wander over to the Blues and on up Tiger Canyon. We'd get a good view of our town and see how it looks now."

"Yeah!" Willie yelled. "Martha, go make some sandwiches so we can stay a long time."

She returned with the sandwiches in a few minutes. They took their time, stopping to enjoy everything they saw.

They ate their sandwiches sitting on an overhang at Tiger Canyon, a huge canyon with trees growing all the way down the steep banks, making a lovely view. They stopped at a gurgling creek to quench their thirst and headed home.

"What a way to welcome spring," Abe said. "I'm ready to start the spring plowing. Are you, Willie?"

"Can I, Abe? I can make those horses go."

As they rambled toward home Abe and Willie figured how he could help drive the big horses. They arrived home just after the warm sunshine turned pink and the sun melted into the horizon.

"We're home, Nellie," Martha called as she hurried into the main room. "We had a great day. You should have come with us. It was warm and smelled of pine needles."

Nellie didn't respond.

"Nellie, where are you?" Martha called, hurrying into Nellie's room. The room looked strangely empty. Then Martha noticed all of Nellie's things were gone from the pegs on the wall. The baby! Martha rushed to the cradle, leaned over, and looked in. The breath she had been holding returned in a whoosh. Babykins lay sleeping soundly in the cradle.

Martha ran back to the main room. "Abe, for a moment I thought Nellie had gone somewhere, but Babykins is asleep in there." Then she remembered Nellie's things missing from the nails. "I wonder where she went," she said.

Abe went outside and returned in five minutes. "Her mare's gone," he said. "And I haven't seen Josie. I guess they're all together. I can't believe she left Babykins alone, even for a little while." He peered into Martha's eyes. "She shouldn't have done that, should she?"

Martha shook her head. "No, you never leave babies

alone, even for a few minutes. Bad things can happen to babies in a hurry."

Babykins stirred, then almost instantly burst into full blown wailing, screaming at the top of her lungs. Martha headed for the bedroom. "Something's wrong," she said. "Babykins has never cried like that before. She barely fusses." When she picked up the baby she seemed all right but searched frantically for something to eat. Martha carried her into the main room.

"She's starved. Abe, how long do you suppose Nellie's been gone?" She jiggled the baby, changing her from one arm to the other. Then she changed the soaked diaper, but that didn't help either.

"I'll go look for Nellie," Abe said. "This is not the way a responsible mother treats her baby. Or the people she's staying with."

Martha walked the baby, rocked the baby, and talked to the baby. She did everything she could think of to get the baby's attention, but Babykins wasn't interested in anything in the world except filling her stomach with warm milk.

Abe returned in half an hour. "She's not close around," he said, talking loudly so Martha could hear him over Babykins' screaming. "It's pitch dark, not even a moon. But I covered the town and a few miles out on each side." He plopped onto the settle. His face looked positively haggard. "You—you don't think she's taken off, do you?"

Instantly Martha saw in her mind the empty nails in Nellie's room. Surely she hadn't gone after Jackson! Her terrified eyes met Abe's. She nodded. "I'll bet she has. Abe! What are we going to do with the baby? I can't nurse her!"

After waiting and listening to Babykins scream for another hour, Martha dissolved some sugar in a little warm water. Then she dipped a clean cloth in it and put the cloth in the baby's mouth. The baby clamped onto it and sucked as if she'd never had anything to eat in her life. After she'd sucked the cloth dry, Martha dipped it again and offered it to the frantic baby.

"Abe, would you go ask Tom what we should do?" she asked while the baby emptied the cloth again.

Abe left and Martha noticed the blessed quiet. She'd had no idea the baby could cry like that. She had always cared for her at the first fuss. "You poor little girl," she cooed to the wildly sucking baby. She fed the child three more clothfuls of sugar water before Abe returned. Tom and Rachel came with him.

"Too bad I don't have a baby," Rachel said. "I nursed all three of mine at once for awhile." she sighed. "But maybe that's why I lost my milk so soon. I'd like to still be nursing the twins."

"You'll have to give her cow's milk if Nellie doesn't come back," Tom said. "Do you think she's really gone?"

"I don't know where she'd be around here," Martha said. "Or how she could go off and leave her baby alone." She shook her head, still holding the cloth for the baby to suck. Finally she nodded. "Yes, I do think she's gone."

"Well, cow's milk is wonderful—for baby cows," Tom said. Then he grinned. "But Babykins won't be the first baby to make do with it. Do you have a baby bottle?" When Martha said no, he sent Abe to the store after one. "Now, you'd better write this down. Put one cup milk, one cup water, and two teaspoons sugar in a small kettle. Bring to boil, cool, and use. Right now that recipe will last her most of the day. It'll keep for a day if it isn't too hot. Later you can double the recipe." He ran his finger down Babykins' soft little cheek. "She'll probably do all right on it. Of course she'll do better on her mother's milk. Let's hope she comes home later tonight."

After Tom and Rachel left, Martha fixed some milk for the baby. Suddenly she missed Josie. Josie wouldn't go off, even if Nellie did—would she? "Abe, are you sure Josie's not around here somewhere?"

twelve

Abe came into the room carrying Babykins over his shoulder. "I haven't seen her, Martha."

Martha dropped her spoon in the milk. "I haven't either, Abe. If she were here, she'd have been jumping all over when the baby cried." Her eyes filled with tears. "Abe, Josie's gone. Something's happened to her. Whatever went on here while we were gone today?"

Abe put one arm around her, still holding the baby over his shoulder. "Nothing really terrible happened, Martha, like something happening to Nellie. We'd have seen signs if it had. Josie went with Nellie, Martha. She didn't know Nellie wasn't coming back."

A smile spread across Martha's gentle, beautiful face. "You're right, Abe. She went with Nellie." Then the smile disappeared. "But she'll never come back, Abe! My Josie, who walked clear across the country with me. I'll never see her again."

"Never's a long time, Martha." He'd better be careful what he said. He would never tell Martha a lie, but he had to make her feel better. "They'll both come back one of these days. You tell me. How could a mother stay away from this beautiful baby?"

Martha didn't look so very convinced, but she put on a brave smile. "Yes. Well, let's try this bottle. I purely hope she'll drink from it." When she took Babykins from Abe, she discovered the baby had fallen asleep. "We better wait until she wakes up," she said. "You're a pretty good father," she added.

Abe barely knew what to think. "That may be what I am," he said, nodding. "I can't believe she really did it. Ran off and left her very own flesh and blood to the mercy of—whoever chooses to take her."

When the baby wakened, she knew exactly what to do to get milk from the bottle and did it with zest. But she fell asleep before she emptied it. Martha had filled it up, not knowing how much Babykins took each time.

Martha and Abe went to bed, still in shock. Were they to be the parents of that little baby forever? Abe couldn't fall asleep. "How about it, Lord?" he asked. "Is Nellie really gone? Is she coming back?"

You're doing fine, Abe.

"Thank You, Lord, but You didn't tell me anything." Abe fell asleep waiting for God to answer.

❧

"Abe, wake up." Abe struggled to open his eyes to a laughing Martha, holding the tiny baby. He sat up and reached for them both. "You don't know how pretty you look with that baby in your arms," he said, hugging them both.

"The baby didn't wake all night," Martha said. "Usually I take her to Nellie twice each night and last night she slept all night. Abe, she's going to do all right on cow's milk."

That afternoon a young woman came to the door with a tiny baby, much younger than Babykins, in her arms. Martha invited her in, then offered coffee. "Would you like some too, Abe?"

Abe looked up from the drawer he was fitting together. "Sure. Why not?"

Martha brought the coffee with cookies. As they ate they

talked about the possible early spring, their homesteads, and how wild the Street was getting.

Finally the young woman cleared her throat. "I heard someone ran off and left her baby with you," she said.

"Yes," Martha said, "my sister-in-law. We're still in shock."

"Well, you can see I have a baby." She looked hard at Martha. "I was wondering if you'd like for me to take the baby and nurse it for a few months? I have way too much milk for one."

Abe felt himself take in a breath. He hadn't been ready for this. Surely Martha wouldn't give up her kin to a stranger to raise.

Martha smiled. "How sweet of you," she said softly.

The woman relaxed. "I couldn't waste my milk while a baby goes hungry, you know."

Martha glanced at Abe, then leaned forward. "But we had a doctor in last night and he told us how to fix cow's milk for the baby. She slept all night. How would it be if we wait and see if she can get along on cow's milk? If she can't handle it, we'll be happy to work out something."

The women went on talking about the babies and their little problems. Abe noticed the woman's baby didn't look nearly as clean as Babykins. He didn't want her taking care of their baby. He just didn't.

After awhile the woman went home. As far as Abe knew Martha hadn't even learned where the woman lived. He nodded his head. Good. They didn't need to know.

When Martha closed the door, Abe pulled her into his arms. "You're a much better mother than that woman. You wouldn't give our baby away, would you?"

Martha shook her head. "Only to save her life," she said. "Then I'd take Babykins to her for each feeding and bring her back. Even if it took every minute of my day."

Abe knew that. Why had he let himself get so worried? "I'm glad, my little Martha. I wouldn't have liked to put her into that woman's care. Or anyone's care but yours."

The baby slept all night again. "I'm sure she's going to be all right," Martha said. "I'm so happy, Abe." She searched his eyes. "How do you feel about all my kin expecting you to care for them? First Willie. We know he'll be with us until he grows up. Now this little baby. Do you feel pushed, Abe?"

How could he explain how he felt? "I'm the luckiest man in the world, Martha. I never think of Willie as your kin. He's as much mine as yours. And I already love this baby. I can see it's going to be hard keeping a baby and loving it like our own, never knowing when its parents might take it away from us. But that problem isn't just mine. We share it, Martha."

The baby seemed perfectly contented on her new formula and was much too young to miss her mother. Besides Martha had always done everything for her except nurse her.

The next morning when the baby fussed, Martha heated the bottle while Abe rocked her. As he held her, talking to her, she watched him intently. A moment later her mouth turned up in a beautiful baby smile. "Martha! Come quick!"

Martha tore into the bedroom. "What happened? Is she all right?"

Abe pulled her to him. "Watch this." He began talking quietly to the little girl who listened carefully, her eyes never leaving his. But he couldn't coax another smile from her. He looked up at Martha. "She smiled at me, Martha. A real smile."

"Don't worry, Abe," Martha said. "She'll do it again."

She smiled again the next day and then often and easily.

❧

A few days later Abe heard a strange sound at the door. Almost like the baby whimpering. He went to see what was out there.

When he opened the door a thin, scraggly dog struggled to its feet. "Josie!" Abe yelled. He threw the door open. "Come in, girl. Martha! Josie's here!"

Martha came running with the baby in her arms. When she saw Josie, she handed the baby to Abe and threw herself to the floor, hugging the dog. Tears ran down her cheeks as she talked to Josie. "Where have you been, baby? Oh, Josie, you don't know how I've missed you." Josie licked Martha's face and lay down on the floor. Martha looked up at Abe. "Where did you find her? Where's she been? What happened, Abe?"

Watching Josie flop down to the floor, Abe thought she looked weak. Bad weak. "I think Josie's hungry, Martha," he said. "She just came to the door. That's all I know, but you better get something for her to eat. She's come a long way."

Martha soon set a plate of meat, potatoes, and gravy before the dog. Josie opened her mouth and inhaled the food in a few gulps. Then she wagged her dirty tail and lay back down. She would probably be all right, but right now she didn't look so good.

"She looks near as bad as when I first met the two of you," he said. "I wish she could tell us where she's been."

"Yes," Martha said. "Then we'd know what happened to Nellie too."

❧

Martha spent the next week caring for the baby and feeding

Josie back into strength and health. Every day Martha and Abe talked about Nellie, wondering if she'd show up and take the baby. Abe told Martha that Nellie had gone far away. He knew because Josie had obviously gone far too.

As Abe worked on his furniture he thought what a precious family he had. Martha must be the best woman in town. Josie was getting stronger each day. Willie was growing to quite a young man, almost eight now. And then there was Babykins. *Babykins! What a thing to call a beautiful baby girl. We'd better give her a name before she thinks she's Babykins.*

"Martha?"

Martha scurried in from their bedroom where she'd been bathing the baby. She held the tiny girl in her arms, wrapped in a large yellow towel. "Did you call, Abe?"

He got up from the floor where he'd been working. "Yes, I was just thinking we need to name Babykins, proper-like."

Martha laughed. "You interrupted her bath for that? Don't you think she could get along without a name for another ten minutes?"

Oh. He hadn't thought. He pulled Martha to him for a quick kiss. "Sure. You go finish the bath. But you might be thinkin' about a name. It's gotta be sweet and pure and beautiful just like her."

Martha sat on the rocker and wrapped the towel tighter around the baby. "I was just joking, Abe. I'd finished her bath and was drying her when you called. Your timing was perfect. I bet you have a name in mind."

He shook his head. "Not really. But she does need a name. Have you been thinkin' on it, Martha?"

She wiped a drop of water from the tip of Babykins' dark hair with the corner of the towel. "Not really Abe. Well, a little bit. I think Kathleen's really pretty. Or Rebecca or Elizabeth or Nellie."

Abe thought a moment. He liked all of them except Nellie. *What is this, Lord? Do I dislike the name Nellie because I don't want to remember Babykins has any parents besides us?*

Be careful, Abe. Nellie and Jackson are real.

We don't have to name the baby Nellie, do we, Lord?

Rebecca's a nice name.

Abe couldn't believe his ears—or his heart—wherever it was he heard God's voice. God had just named the baby! Better get that other question in real quick. *Lord, do You want us to build a new house? We'll need a bigger one with our family growin' like it is.*

"Abe! You started this conversation. Now you're daydreaming so bad you don't even hear me," Martha scolded.

Abe turned his attention to Martha with a start. Then a big grin covered his face. "The Lord just named the baby. Think Rebecca's all right?"

A lovely sweet look came over Martha as she smiled. "I love the name, Abe. I purely love it." She raised her eyes. "Thank You, Lord for naming our baby. Rebecca's the prettiest name of all. Help us take the best care of her, Lord, and teach her to love You as we do. We ask in Jesus' name and thank You. Amen."

Abe moved beside Martha, then dropped to his knees beside the rocker and touched the baby's hair. "Hello, little Rebecca," he said softly. "You really look like a Rebecca."

Martha put her hand on Abe's as he touched the baby. Suddenly her eyes opened wide. "Abe! What's her last name? Does it have to be Lawford? Or can it be Noble?"

Abe hadn't thought that far. Lawford. Noble. Finally he

grinned. "We could say she was born to us."

Martha returned his grin. "We could—but we couldn't. You know where the Good Book says all liars end up."

"Yeah. I didn't mean it. I wonder if Tom would know."

They hurried over to Tom and Rachel's place, Martha carrying the baby and Abe watching Willie and Josie race around them. They found Rachel busy making a cake. Two cakes.

"I was just going to send Melissa over to invite you to the twins' first birthday party," she said. "We'll have cake and rice pudding with whipped cream. I made one chocolate cake and one white so they can make a great mess at the party. Tommy will too, for that matter."

"I suppose Tom's busy," Abe said.

"He's out in the office, I think," Rachel said. "Unless someone's dragged him off to see a patient." Then her eyes became concerned. "Is Babykins all right?"

"She's fine," Martha said. "But her name's not Babykins anymore. The Lord just named her Rebecca. We were wondering if Tom would know what her last name would be, ours or Nellie and Jackson's?"

Rachel smiled and shoved a red curl behind her ear with a chocolaty finger. "He might know, but if he does it's not because he's a doctor. Let's go see if he's in the office."

Martha, Abe, Willie, and Rebecca followed Rachel to the office. Josie stayed beside the door. They found two people sitting in the entry room who told them the doctor was with someone else right now.

They all sat down on a leather davenport to wait. Just then someone banged hard on the office door. Rachel ran and opened it. Tommy came in. "Mama come. Jesse cry. Fa' down."

Rachel turned to Martha, grinning. "Gotta go. My little keepers keep close tabs on me. Come back to the house after you see Tom."

⁂

Tom didn't know much about things like Abe and Martha were dealing with. "Why don't you find a lawyer? If you can't you might look up the judge. They ought to know what the law says about it."

They thanked him, stuck their heads in the door, and told Rachel good-bye, then headed for the Street. They knew there were lawyers in town because they'd advertised in *The Statesman*, but they hadn't had occasion to need one.

They walked west on the Street until Abe spotted a sign, ADAM JENSEN, ATTORNEY AT LAW. "Isn't that a lawyer?" he asked.

Martha smiled. "I think so. Why don't they all call themselves the same thing?"

On going in, they found a thin blond man with a bushy mustache sitting at a small round table writing on a tablet. He stood and nodded. "Adam Jensen, at your service." He motioned to chairs on the other side of the table, which they took.

"We've some questions about our baby here," Abe said. He told the man exactly what had happened and what they wanted to know.

"How long's the mother been gone?" Jensen asked. They told him a month. He shook his head. "Not long enough. The only way you can legally change the baby's name is to adopt her. If the mother doesn't come back in five more months I'd go ahead and draw up adoption papers. 'Course you can call her by your name now. Won't matter 'tall."

"I want my name to be Noble too," Willie cried.

Abe nearly jumped at Willie's outburst. He'd had no idea the boy even listened to the discussion. Suddenly he recognized how Willie felt. He would be the only one in the family with a different name. No one wants to be different. He turned back to the lawyer. "Well, let's let Willie's name be Noble. Isn't anyone to object to that. His parents are dead."

The attorney started asking questions and writing on the pad. When he'd asked about nearly every iota of their private life, he smiled. "Sounds good. Won't really make any difference whether you adopt him, he's yours anyway. Could just change his name."

"No! I want Abe to 'dopt me!"

Abe grinned. "Let's go for the adoption."

The attorney wrote up several papers while Abe and Martha waited, Rebecca rested, and Willie wiggled.

When he finished, Jensen reached out a hand to Willie. Willie put his hand in the big one. "Congratulations, Willie," the attorney said. "You're legally Mr. and Mrs. Noble's son. You can call them Papa and Mama now."

Willie burst out laughing. "No! They're Martha and Abe. Is my name Noble now?"

Jensen assured him it was.

Abe paid the man and the family started out the door. "Come back in a few months if the mother doesn't show up," Jensen said.

ॐ

Martha laughed out loud as they walked toward home. "That didn't turn out the way we expected, did it?"

"No," Abe said, "but it turned out great. Don't you think? We have a happy boy, who won't be on the outside now if we do adopt Rebecca."

Everyone fussed for food when they got home, and Rebecca got her tummy filled first. She always took her bottle with joy and excitement, thinking it was the perfect food.

After dinner, Abe worked on a table and chair set for an eager family, while Martha cleaned the house and did a washing. The baby slept.

Later in the afternoon Abe grew restless. He needed to do something different. Something to take his mind off Nellie, and what she might do. Martha looked as if she had finished her heavy work. She sat in a chair mending Willie's pants.

Suddenly a ride sounded good to him. Out in the fresh air. He sat down in the chair across from Martha. "Are you tired of that?" he asked.

She looked up with a question in her eyes, then joy. "Of what, Abe? I'm never tired of doing for my family."

"Well, the horses need some exercise. And so do I."

She laid her work aside, got up, and started to get her coat. Then she stopped and looked at Abe. "How am I going to ride? We have a baby now."

Abe had forgotten all about that. Nellie had been here before when they rode, so she watched the baby. "You're going to ride, Martha. We'll think of something. Think someone could keep the baby?"

Martha shook her head. "Everyone's busy, Abe. We better figure it out ourselves. I wonder if I could make some sort of papoose board."

Abe thought that a great idea. "Martha, you said it! Let's go get one from the Indians. They must have an extra one around somewhere."

Willie and Abe soon had the horses saddled, warm coats on everyone, and Rebecca wrapped in a heavy blanket. Abe helped Martha up, then handed the baby to her. "This'll work just fine until we get the papoose board," Martha said. "I suppose I shouldn't do anything too reckless though."

"When we get the papoose board can we go for a good ride?" Willie asked.

"You bet," Abe agreed. "We'll let the horses go as fast as they want." The three turned the horses west toward Fort Walla Walla and the little Indian village, and plodded sedately along. After a half hour Abe saw the trees and large buildings at the Fort. A moment later they drew near the little tepee village.

But three horses standing impatiently by the trail ahead caught Abe's interest. As they neared he saw several people rolling around on the ground. He nudged Ebb who understood exactly and sped up his walk. When they got close, Abe saw two white men beating an Indian with big clubs. He jumped off Ebb, dropped the reins, and ran behind the white men. "Drop the clubs," he yelled loudly, as he slipped his right hand in his pocket. "Now! I have three bullets for each of you, and I'll deliver as soon as I get this said!"

The clubs dropped to the ground, the men looked around, and the Indian tried to struggle to his feet. As Abe picked up the clubs, he recognized Camas. "What's goin' on here?" he asked the white men.

Camas made a small sound, and Abe looked at him. Blood dripped from the young Indian's nose and a wound on his forehead. Those men hadn't been playing a game. The Indian pointed to the white men. "Take gold," he said. Abe didn't understand. Camas tried again. "Take Abe's gold!"

thirteen

Martha heard and understood. These were two of the men who'd taken their gold, the men the Indians had stolen the gold back from—as well as the thieves' horses and guns. She started to yell at Abe, to explain what happened, when she could tell he also understood.

He snapped to attention, keeping his right hand in his coat pocket. "All right, you two, throw down your fire arms. Now! We been stringin' up vermin like you around here. Lots of 'em. My finger's mighty nervous, dealin' with the likes of you."

"We ain't got no guns. Why'd you think we was usin' clubs on that savage? Them sneaks took our guns too."

Abe seemed to accept that. "All right, get on your horses with no funny stuff." The men moved toward their horses. "Martha, you cover the one on the brown horse. I'll watch the white horse."

Martha almost giggled. Neither of them had a gun. Abe didn't believe in carrying one. Said some innocent person was more apt to get hurt than the one breaking the law. "All right, Abe," she answered. "I've got him."

"Head toward the Street," Abe ordered. "The law's about halfway down. You're on your way to jail. You boys don't know how lucky you are. Most people around are dishing out their own justice when they come across the likes of you."

The men didn't say a word, just turned their horses in a northeast direction. Abe, Martha, and Willie rode behind them.

When they reached the Street the men turned east, went a few blocks, and stopped beside the sheriff's building and jail. Abe bailed off Ebb in a hurry. "Get off those horses. Easy-like." The men did, their hands raised.

"Get movin' right through that door," Abe instructed. The men started toward the door, but the sheriff met them before they reached it.

"What's goin' on, Abe?" he asked.

"Caught these boys killin' an Indian," Abe ground through his teeth.

"Where's the Injun?" the sheriff wanted to know.

Martha inhaled hard. She'd forgotten all about Camas. She looked at Abe to find him staring at her. He'd forgotten too. *Please, Lord, help Camas to be all right. Thank You in Jesus' name, Father. Amen.*

Abe flashed a sickly grin at the sheriff. "Guess we forgot all about him. He was bleedin' from the nose and also a cut on his head where these varmints tried to beat him to death with clubs. Two on one, even."

The sheriff waved his gun at the men. "Go on in there." When they got inside, the sheriff told them to sit on some chairs near a table. When they got settled, he sat in a chair in front of them. "Wha'd that redskin do to you boys?" he asked softly.

One of the men took a deep breath and gave Abe a long look. "They stole our gold and our horses," he said. "We seen this savage on one of our horses so we decided to take it back. We'd a gotten it too, if that fool who thinks he's God's little helper hadn't a come along."

The sheriff looked at Abe, his eyebrows up.

Oh, God, Martha prayed silently, *show Abe what to say. Thank You, Father. In Jesus' name.*

Abe moved to the table the men sat around. "I reckon the good Lord brought us to that spot today. Fact is, we happened to be with the Indians when those two with two others robbed the Indians' gold last spring. A couple days later the Indians found them in a drunken stupor and took their gold back. They took the horses too, for self-protection. We'd a' all been shot dead before we got home if they hadn't taken the horses." Abe held up his right hand. "As God is my witness, that's exactly what happened."

The sheriff turned back to the men. "That what happened?"

The men spit out a few curse words before one answered. "No, that ain't what happened. They just came upon us whilst we was sleepin' and took the horses. We had to walk a hunnert miles. Carried the saddles half that way, then dumped 'em."

"No gold involved?" Abe asked the men.

The men looked at each other for several seconds, their eyes wide. "No gold," the man answered. "Just horses." He turned back to the sheriff. "I hear you punish horse thieves quick and harsh in this town. You best go get the Indian before his kin rescue him."

The sheriff appeared to study the matter. Then he turned to Abe. "I don't rightly know what to do, Abe. The men deny your charges."

"Look, Sheriff," Abe said. "They've admitted enough for you to know they're the ones involved. You heard him say the Indians took their gold and horses. When I asked him point blank if there was gold involved he denied it. He's lyin' through his teeth. And they can't deny tryin' to kill the Indian today. Lock 'em up. Take 'em to court to find out if they're guilty. That's what trials are for."

Thank You, Lord, Martha said silently. *You gave Abe all he needed.*

The sheriff lumbered to his feet and waved a gun at the two men. "Well, I guess you got free room and board fer tonight. We'll sort through this tomorrow."

Abe turned to Martha. "Let's go get Tom and take him to check Camas."

A half hour later they discovered Camas gone. "Someone hauled him off to a tepee," Abe said. "Right over here, Tom."

Gray Wolf met them before they reached the tepees. He held his hand out to Abe. "Abe good," he said.

"Thanks, Gray Wolf. Camas?" He pointed to Tom. "Doctor."

Gray Wolf, looking relieved, turned and led them to a tepee behind his. He pointed, turned, and returned to his own home.

Abe called Camas' name. A pretty Indian woman opened the flap and motioned them in. Martha and Willie went in first, then Abe and Tom brought up the rear. Camas, who'd been cleaned up, lay on a pallet on the floor of the smoky tent. The place smelled like fish-oil mixed with food and smoke. Martha remembered Willie beside her and Rebecca in her arms. "Abe," she said softly. "We'll wait outside for you." He nodded to show he had heard, so she led Willie out.

"Doesn't it smell good out here?" Willie asked right away.

"Yes. That's why I brought you out. But since we're out, let's see if Gray Wolf knows anything about papoose boards."

Gray Wolf responded to her first soft call. "Camas?" he asked.

She shook her head. "I don't know, Gray Wolf. They're looking at him now."

"Doctor fix Camas?"

"He'll try." How could she change the subject to something

as frivolous as papoose boards?

But Gray Wolf did it for her. He pointed at the sleeping baby. "Martha papoose?"

Martha laughed to herself. Gray Wolf and his sons came often for food, English lessons, and Bible lessons. He must know tummies get big before little ones come along. "No. Martha keep papoose." Now was the time. "Martha need papoose board," she said. Seeing he didn't understand she said, "Papoose board." She motioned to her back, as if putting the baby back there. Gray Wolf looked carefully at her back but didn't seem to understand. "Put papoose there," she said, leaning over and forming a board on her back.

Suddenly Gray Wolf's eyes brightened. "Papoose Martha back," he patted Martha's back.

Maybe he was getting it! "Martha need papoose on back," she said. "Gray Wolf help?"

Gray Wolf thought a moment. "Gray Wolf help?" he repeated. Martha nodded yes.

"Come Gray Wolf." Martha followed the tall Indian toward another tepee.

He stopped at a dark-colored one and called softly. His usually coarse voice sounded almost like a bird. A tall Indian woman came out and Gray Wolf pointed to Martha and the baby, then said a few words in the Nez Percé language. Martha understood some of them. One was "give." He must be planning to give it to her. Oh well, how do you pay an Indian who has a whole cave full of gold?

The Indian woman ran lightly between the tepees until she disappeared. Gray Wolf turned back to Martha. "Come back," he said.

The woman did come back in a few minutes. She held exactly what Martha needed. A pretty papoose case made from light and dark leather. The woman handed it to Martha. "Thank you," Martha told the woman. She repeated it to Gray Wolf two or three times. Then she handed it to him and pointed to her back. He took it and laid it on the ground. Then he took the baby, put her into it, and laced it up tight so she wouldn't slump down. Rebecca didn't awaken. Not even when Gray Wolf strapped it on Martha's back. It felt good to Martha, and her tired arms rejoiced. She turned this way and that, jumping just a little. Rebecca slept on. Martha thanked Gray Wolf again and again.

"Abe fix Camas," he said every time she thanked him. She had prayed for Camas to be all right, but she decided to do it again with Gray Wolf. She pointed up. "Abe's God fix Camas."

She kneeled on the ground and pulled him down beside her. Willie dropped to the ground on her other side. Martha put her arm over Willie's shoulders. "Dear Father," she said. "We thank You for Your great love for us and for forgiving our sins. Because You love us so very much, we love You, too, Father, more than life. Now, Father, we ask You in Jesus' name to help Camas get well right away. Thank You, Father. Amen."

In less than a minute, Abe came out of the tent. "How is he?" Martha asked.

"He's hurt bad, but we asked God to help. He'll be all right."

Gray Wolf hadn't understood much. "Camas?"

Abe pointed upward. "Big God help Camas get well."

Gray Wolf understood that. He nodded. "Camas get well."

A grin spread over Abe's face. Martha wondered what he'd thought of. He pointed into the sky again. "Big God bring Abe and Martha here today. So we help Camas."

Gray Wolf thought a moment, then he relaxed and nodded. "Big God bring Abe." He peered at Abe. "Gray Wolf thank big God."

Abe looked at Martha. She nodded. "Let's kneel before our big God," Abe said, "and thank Him for bringing Abe and Martha here. And for helping Camas get well." They did, then got to their feet. Martha saw Gray Wolf wipe a tear from his eye. Either he loved God a lot or he still feared for Camas' life.

Abe noticed the papoose board on Martha's back and moved over to have a look. "That looks pretty good," he said. "Now you won't drop her when you ride. Hey, you'll be able to work in the garden too."

"Yes. That's partly why I needed it so bad. She likes it too."

Abe pulled some money from his pocket and turned to Gray Wolf. "Let me pay you for the papoose board."

Gray Wolf backed up. "Abe God make Camas well."

Tom came from Camas's tent. "Is he going to be all right?" Martha asked.

Tom looked tired but peaceful. "When I first saw him I wasn't sure, but something happened since then. He's much better." He grinned. "Could have something to do with our great God." He turned to Martha. "Would you stop and tell Rachel I'm staying with him tonight? At least for a while, just in case.

Martha, Abe, Willie, and Rebecca on Martha's back mounted their horses and prepared to leave. Gray Wolf seemed unwilling for them to go, hanging around even when they wanted to start.

Suddenly Abe jumped from his horse. "Something wrong, Gray Wolf?" he asked the older man.

Gray Wolf turned to face Camas's tent. "Doctor?" he said with a question in his voice. "Doctor big God man?"

"Yes!" Abe nearly bellowed. "The doctor is our big God's man. Our big God will help Tom, Gray Wolf."

Gray Wolf reached out an arm and patted Abe's back. "Good. Abe go."

"Thank you for the papoose board," Martha called as they rode away.

They stopped and told Rachel Tom wouldn't be home for a while, maybe not until morning, and went home weary but happy.

The next morning Martha gave away many gallons of milk. More people seemed to hear about it, for more came every day. Then Abe took the rest to the Street to sell. He couldn't bring enough to satisfy the merchants with the expanded population.

After they finished the necessary tasks, Abe asked Martha if she would like to try out her papoose board on a walk to the jail. "I want to see what's going on," he said. "I wouldn't be surprised if they turned those two loose and arrested Camas."

But they hadn't been turned loose. "I really ain't got much reason to keep 'em," the sheriff said. "Seems to be one person's word against the other's. Knowing them redskins like I do, I'd likely believe the two we got here."

Martha felt fear, then remembered God. *Make this turn out right, Father*, she prayed silently. Peace filled her being.

Abe looked as serene as Rebecca on Martha's back. "You know me too, Sheriff. Ever known me to tell something that isn't true?"

The man spit on the floor. "Well, can't say as I have, but

you ain't God. You could be mistaken."

"Buckley! You heard them change their story last night when I asked about gold. When people tell the truth they don't have to do that. You'd better start working up a case against them. If you turn them loose, I'm gonna make you more trouble 'n you ever saw. Come on, Martha."

As they walked back home, Martha thanked God again for Abe. *He's purely your man, Father,* she ended.

"Let's get the horses," Abe said. "I can't wait to see how Camas is. We owe Willie a good ride, too."

"Yea!" Willie said. "Let's take sandwiches."

"You just want an excuse to eat," Martha told him.

After feeding Rebecca and making sandwiches, they saddled the horses and headed west. As they dismounted, Martha noticed an Indian limping toward them. Camas! She ran and hugged him carefully. "Tom made you better!" she said.

Camas shook his head and pointed a finger skyward. "Big God make well."

"You're right," she said, laughing. "People can't make you well, but our big God can."

Gray Wolf came out, so they all thanked the big God together. Then Abe led his little family on a nice ride in the early spring sunshine. As they rode Martha kept thinking how nice the papoose board was. Why didn't white people make something like that to use? They stopped to eat sandwiches, then returned home.

Abe began sanding on a chair to go with the table he'd just finished for a new family in town. "How many chairs do you have to make?" Martha asked, thinking chairs looked harder than tables to make, with all those small pieces to cut, shape, sand, and finish.

Abe looked up at her and grinned. "Only seven more after this one. If I'd stay home and work, I'd get them done in a few days."

Martha fed the baby, put her to bed, and started mixing up bread. When she had everything in it and was kneading the big batch of dough, she decided to ask something she'd been thinking about. "When can we start working outside?" she asked. "We've been outside a lot lately. Looks like we're having an early spring—and we had a glorious winter. Abe, isn't God truly good to us?"

"He is, Martha." Abe chuckled. "I been thanking Him a lot for that baby in there. I think He arranged for us to have her, knowin' how much we both wanted a baby."

Martha smiled. "I been thinking about that too, Abe. But He could have given us one of our very own just as easily. He'd never cause all the heartache involved for us to have Rebecca." She shook her head as she turned dough and pushed it and turned it again. "Never, Abe. He's a God of love."

"You're right, Martha, but He can make good come out of bad things. I reckon I'll just keep thankin' Him."

"Me too, Abe. Me too." She gathered up the lively mass of dough and dumped it back into the bowl, spread a cloth over it, and put it on a shelf over the cook stove to rise.

Later that afternoon Willie came running into the house where Martha scrubbed baby clothes. "Martha, a man just rode by on a horse. He asked me if Nellie Lawford is my kin. I said yes and he said he saw her yesterday."

Martha dropped the diaper she held. "Where did he see her?" she asked.

Willie shook his head. "I don't know. He didn't tell me that."

She grabbed Willie by his shoulders. "Where's the man, Willie? I have to talk to him."

"He's gone, Martha. I told you he was riding a horse—a big gray horse with brown spots. He stopped only a minute to talk to me. Then he just kept going."

Martha dropped her hands from Willie's shoulders and raced outside. She looked east, then west. Not a horse and man in sight—not even a horse or a man. She ran back inside. "Willie, tell me what the man looked like."

"I don't know, Martha," Willie said. "I saw the horse though. I told you what the horse looked like."

fourteen

Get hold of yourself, Martha, she told herself. She took a deep breath. And another. Willie had done everything right. He couldn't have done more, even if he had noticed what the man looked like. She pulled Willie onto her lap. "I'm sorry I got so excited," she whispered into his ear. "You did everything exactly right."

Abe walked into the house. "Abe!" Willie yelled, "a man went by and told me he saw Nellie."

Abe dropped to his knees before Willie, still on Martha's lap. "Where is she?" he asked.

"The man's gone. He had a gray horse with brown spots."

Abe looked at Martha. He had never seen her looking so stricken. "What happened?"

She shook her head. "That's all we know, Abe. The man stopped just long enough to tell Willie. I ran out but didn't see a thing." Her lips formed a shaky grin. "At least the horse was unusual. If we ever see a horse like that we could ask."

"Yeah." Abe got up. "Come on, Willie. Let's get the horses saddled. We're goin' for a ride." He lifted his eyes to Martha. "Get Rebecca ready." Then he took Willie's hand and together they went outside.

As they saddled the horses, Abe noticed how much real help Willie was becoming. He felt as though just yesterday he'd made Willie think he was helping, but now the boy grabbed cinches and tightened them, put on bridles, and most anything.

145

When they finished, they led the horses to the house. Martha waited in front of the house with Rebecca strapped on her back.

Abe jumped from his saddle and helped Martha and Rebecca up. Martha gave him a radiant smile. "Where are we going, Abe?"

Her words surprised Abe. He'd figured she would know. "We're headed for Jackson's place. Maybe she just went home—and forgot to get Rebecca."

When they rode up to the house it didn't look very lived in. But he wasn't going to leave until he knew for sure. He slid from the saddle, moved to Thunder's side, and held his arms to Martha. "Come on, we're goin' in." He turned to Willie. "You comin'? Let's go see what's goin' on."

As they approached the door, Abe wondered why he'd pushed this confrontation. Maybe if they had just left it alone, Nellie would never have come after Rebecca. Willie banged his fist loudly on the door when they stood in front of it. No one answered. Abe knocked. Still no response. Abe noticed his breathing had nearly stopped as they waited in silence.

After another minute he drew in a deep breath. "I'm goin' in," he said, pulling the latch. "It's locked. Now what? Are we givin' up?" He looked to Martha for her response. She shrugged. "I'm for breakin' in," he said. "Nellie could be in there sick or worse."

Willie ran around the house and returned almost immediately. "The back doors hangin' open, Abe. Come on."

Abe grinned. "Why didn't I think of goin' in the back, Willie?" He held a hand to Martha. "Come on. We're goin' to see if she's here or if she's been here." He studied her face. "Think we can tell if she's been here?"

"I'm not sure. I didn't look around much when we took

her home."

"Well, come on," Willie said. "If we go in we'll soon find out."

Willie led the way into the kitchen part of the main room. Abe noticed how clean and neat it looked. He met Martha's eyes. "Did it look this neat when we left with Nellie?"

She shook her head. "I haven't the faintest idea. Let's look through the house a little."

They found a few of Nellie's clothes in the bedroom and also a pair of Jackson's overalls. None of them knew if they'd been there before. Abe checked the fireplace. It was cold with hardly any ashes. He had no idea how long it had been since it held a fire.

They closed the back door as they left, knowing little more than when they came.

"Let's go ask at Fort Walla Walla about the horse," Abe suggested. Letting the horses have their heads, they turned west.

⅔

The soldier nodded at Abe's question. "Yes, we sold a horse like that. It's been over six months, probably near a year now. I have no idea who bought it."

Abe leaned toward the man. "This is important, sir. Do you have records you could check?"

The man invited them in and offered them chairs while he searched for the information. After a long fifteen-minute wait an army officer approached. "We found the information you're looking for," he said. "But you'd better tell us why you want to find the man."

Abe looked at Martha. She smiled. "Sure," Abe said. "I don't mind at all." He explained about Jackson and Nellie disappearing. He pointed at Rebecca on Martha's back and explained they had left the baby. And that a man riding that horse had told Willie he had seen Nellie.

The man nodded. "Just wanted to be sure everything was all right. The man's name is Wallace Dugan. That's all I have. He didn't have an address at the time. Says here he was taking out a donation land claim."

"Wallace Dugan," Abe repeated. "That oughta be some help. Much obliged, sir."

When they reached the thriving little town of Walla Walla, Abe said, "I'm gonna check on the Street."

"I have to go home, Abe," Martha said. "Rebecca's starting to wiggle. She's overtime for her feeding so in a minute she'll let the whole world know."

"You go on," Abe said. "I'll just ask around a little."

When Abe entered Galbraith's Saloon, the owner looked surprised. "Ain't seen you for a while, Abe. Thought maybe you was too good fer me nowadays."

Abe grinned and sat down at the counter. "You know better'n that. If you had a wife could cook like mine you wouldn't eat out much either. Bring me a coffee and sandwich."

While he ate, Abe asked Galbraith, his faithful old friend, if he knew the man, Wallace Dugan. Galbraith shook his head. "He's been in but not for awhile. Probably got a wife. Them women beat me out of a lot of business."

"Know where he lives?"

Galbraith grinned. "I barely know where you live. Only reason I have any idea atall is 'cause you came when there weren't nobody here yet." He whistled. "So many people here now, can't even tell which ones're your friends."

"You're right," Abe said, shoving in the last bite of sandwich. He got up. "Gotta find that man one way or another. See you later."

His next stop was at the sheriff's office. "I hoped I

wouldn't have to look at your face today," the man said. "I still got 'em locked up. Got a lawyer goin' over the facts too, to see if we need to take these boys to trial."

"Sounds like you're doing good," Abe said. "Right now I wonder if you know a Wallace Dugan."

The sheriff squinted his face as he thought. "Can't remember the name, anyway. What's up? He beat up some savages too?"

Abe laughed as he brushed his hair back. "Not that I know of. I just wanted to talk to him on some business. Thanks."

Abe tried several more stores and businesses but finally gave up and went home. After rubbing Ebb down and releasing him in the corral, he went inside. Maybe he could finish that chair today.

"Why were we looking so hard for that man?" Martha asked when he went in.

Suddenly Abe didn't really know. He grinned sheepishly. "I'm not sure. I know it's not because we want to get rid of Rebecca. Could it be that we're terrified for Nellie to be in town?"

Martha touched Rebecca's soft little cheek as the baby sucked vigorously on her bottle. "I'm purely in love with her already, Abe. I don't think I want to know any more about Nellie. Ever. I could hardly stand it when we went looking for her."

Abe nodded. He understood the feeling. "I know. I really didn't want to, but I thought we had to. You know, face the enemy. Never let him sneak up behind you."

"Maybe we should move away, Abe. Somewhere where they could never find us."

For a second Abe thought that a great idea. But he shook his head. "We have to do the right thing, Martha. I'd like to do that too, but that's almost running from the law. We'd be looking over our shoulder the rest of our lives."

Martha looked sad. "We're going to be doing that anyway, Abe."

"No. Remember that attorney, Jensen, said we could adopt her in six months? Then she'll be ours, Martha. Forever. And we won't have to hide."

Relief flooded her eyes. "That's right. So we won't run. We'll just live through it."

Willie had moved to the settle beside Martha. "I'm yours, Martha. I'm yours forever, and you don't have to hide from anyone."

Willie! What did he think about their wild talk about running with Rebecca? Abe sprang to the couch, grabbed Willie and held him tight. "You bet you're ours, Willie. I thank God every day for you too. Today when we were saddling the horses I noticed how you're growin' and gettin' stronger. We're mighty proud of you, Willie."

Martha took it up where Abe left off, telling Willie how proud of him they felt and how much they loved him. The little boy marched off with his head high and his back straight.

The next day someone came with a message for Abe. He took the rumpled piece of paper and read:

> *Abe,*
> *　We're havin' a trial for them boys you*
> *brung in. Tomorrow afternoon in the court*
> *room. Figured you'd want to be there—and*
> *cause a lot of trouble.*
>
> *　　　　　　　　James A. Buckley*
> *　　　　　　　Sheriff Walla Walla County*

"I guess I won't be workin' on chairs tomorrow," Abe

said. "I gotta go and make sure they don't turn it around and put the Indians on trial."

Martha put the last pin in Rebecca's diaper. "I want to be there too, Abe. Think that would be all right?"

"Sure, if Willie can sit still that long." Abe thought a moment. "I think I'll go on down there now and see what they've done."

The sheriff greeted Abe. "Figured you'd never wait 'til tomorrow to get here," he said. "Shoulda waited 'til tomorrow to tell you."

"I'll bet you wish you'd done that, don't you? Well, I was just wondering who the attorneys are."

"Abraham Donovan's prosecutin' them. Got Adam Jensen to defend. That suit ya?"

Abe nodded. "Sounds good. I don't know Donovan, but Jensen seems pretty fair. Did you give him all the information I gave you? Are you callin' any witnesses?"

The sheriff gave Abe a smug look. "You wanta know, come and see." Somehow Abe wasn't quite satisfied with the sheriff's answers. He decided to get Ebb and go see the Indians. They should be at the trial for sure.

The next morning Martha and Abe hurried to get everything done to free up the afternoon. Abe could hardly wait. He expected almost anything to happen, and not necessarily honest things.

Aunt Mandy offered to keep Willie and Rebecca for the afternoon so Abe and Martha could both watch the proceedings carefully. They hurried into the court room at 12:45. People filled the four rows of five chairs each. Twenty people laughing and talking created quite a buzz. The judge, attorneys, sheriff, and prisoners weren't there yet. Neither were the Indians.

Abe and Martha found a place to stand against the west wall.

"Good thing we didn't bring Willie and Rebecca," Abe said.

Then the door in the front of the room opened and the prisoners came in with Adam Jensen. The sheriff and Abraham Donovan came in next and finally the judge. The Indians came in the front door, spotted Abe and Martha along the wall, and joined them.

Sheriff Buckley called the court to order and asked for twelve "staunch law-abiding men to serve on the jury. Men from all around stood up and marched to the special seats that had been saved for them. When they all sat down, they lacked one juror. Abe suggested Gray Wolf go but he didn't. A roughly-dressed middle-aged white man meandered to the last seat.

The judge called the prisoners to the front. "You are charged with beating an Indian with a blunt instrument and inflicting bodily harm. The attorneys will give their talks."

Abraham Donovan opened the case with his speech. "These men were caught in the act of beating a single Indian man severely with clubs. The Indian lay on the ground helpless, but the two prisoners didn't stop. No, they continued beating him with their huge clubs as though surely trying to kill the savage."

The sheriff stood. "The defending lawyer will talk now."

Adam Jensen stood up. "These men have been totally misunderstood, friends. They're the victims in this case. They were merely trying to retrieve their own horse that the Indian had stolen earlier. The man refused to give them their horse, though not denying it to be theirs. Watch and see how it really happened."

"I think Abraham Donovan goes first," the judge said.

Donovan stood and walked to the front again. "The case is pure and simple," he said, "just like I already said. Abram

Noble and his wife came upon the scene and saved the redskin's life. That's all there is to it, gentlemen of the jury. It's your civic duty to find them guilty." He sat down.

Adam Jensen walked to the front. "This is the part of the story you didn't know. The redskin and two of his friends stole four horses from the defendants last summer, leaving the defendants to walk a hundred miles. When they recognized one of their horses they went after it. Wouldn't you? When the savage refused to give it to them they fought for it. Wouldn't you?"

He sat down. Donovan hurried to the front. "I'm sorry, Mr. Jensen. I didn't know about that. I want to drop my case against the gentlemen. I'll move that we—"

Abe tore to the front of the room, interrupting Donovan's motion. "You still don't know what happened, any of you." He scowled at the sheriff. "Except Buckley. I happened to be with the Indians last spring when these men, along with two others attacked. They robbed my good friends, Gray Wolf, Pony Boy, and Camas of all of their gold, lots of gold. They were armed and masked, like any common bandits. A few days later, the Indians luckily found the robbers in a drunken stupor and retrieved their gold. They took the robbers' horses to protect their lives until they got home. The men could have had their horses anytime.

"When they recognized their horse, they didn't demand their horse. They wanted revenge so they tried to kill Camas. They nearly did too. The Indians are here. So is my wife. Ask any of them. Their stories will match mine because mine's true. As God is my witness I swear today that everything I've said here is true."

Abe strode over and stood beside Martha against the wall. Deep silence shrouded the court room. Martha patted Abe's knee. Still no one said anything.

Finally Adam Jensen walked to the front. "Gentlemen," he said, "I feel I've made a grave mistake. Am I correct that Mr. and Mrs. Abram Noble are pillars in our society? The very epitome of integrity? I've heard some of the things they've done to promote honesty and fair play in our town as it grows and develops. I've also talked to the prisoners at length and felt something not quite right. I couldn't put my finger on it so decided I was being prejudiced. But I feel deeply that Abe Noble has just told us the real story as it really happened. I've never knowingly defended guilty men, so I'm withdrawing my services to them immediately."

fifteen

The judge jumped to his feet. "You can't do that, Jensen. The law says everyone gets legal representation. You jest be thinkin' on how you can best do that without crossin' your morals."

Abraham Donovan strode forward. "I think what we need here is to find out exactly what happened. I'm callin' that Injun what got beat to the stand."

Camas didn't move. Martha realized he didn't understand, so she leaned over and told him in simple English mixed with Nez Percé. He looked toward Donovan and shook his head no. Martha smiled. "You have to," she said. Then she took his arm and led him to the front. "Martha stay," she whispered, easing him toward the witness chair.

When Camas stood beside the chair, Marshall Gilliam held up his right hand. "You swear to tell the truth, the whole truth and nuthin' but the truth, so help you God?" he droned.

Camas looked at Martha. She smiled and nodded. "Say yes," she whispered.

Camas looked as though he feared another beating but he met the judge's eyes. "Yes," he said.

The judge looked to Abraham Donovan. "Your witness," he said.

Donovan moved toward Camas. The Indian shrank back into the chair. "It's all right," Martha whispered. "Listen. Maybe you can tell what he says."

"Did you steal that horse from these gentlemen?" Donovan asked.

Camas looked puzzled. Martha stood straight. "Camas take horse?" She pointed toward the accused men.

Camas nodded. "Yes," he said loud and clear. "Camas, Gray Wolf, Pony Boy take four horses."

The corporate gasp nearly made Martha collapse. Camas had just freed the robbers! No! He'd done exactly right. She smiled and nodded at Camas to show him he'd done right.

Donovan strutted before his audience. "I guess we owe our mistakenly arrested friends an apology," he said.

Again Abe bounded to the front. "Wait a minute! This man just told you the truth. Now be a lawyer and get to the bottom of it!"

Donovan looked angry for a moment, then smiled. "I can do that, Mr. Noble, if it'll satisfy you." He faced Camas again. "When did you take the four horses?"

Martha watched Camas and realized he understood. "After men take Indian gold. Much gold. Indians take gold, horses, guns."

Donovan looked at Martha. "You have this savage well-trained, Mrs. Noble. Like a dog doing tricks."

Martha felt her face flush. "Mr. Donovan, why don't you want to learn the truth and deal justice to everyone? These Indian men are totally honest. Ask him anything, but do it in real simple language. I promise he understands your language better than you do his." Several laughs around the court room gave Martha hope.

Abraham Donovan simmered down and worked with Camas. When Camas understood, he answered every question, and none of Donovan's tricks fooled him.

When Donovan quit, the judge asked Jensen if he wanted to question Camas.

"I think they've pretty well answered everyone's questions," Jensen said.

The judge instructed the jury and the men went into the small room the judge indicated.

An hour later, at six o'clock, the jury hadn't come out so the judge instructed everyone to go home. Most did. Martha and Abe waited with the Indians.

At eight o'clock the judge said the verdict would be announced the next morning at eight o'clock. The sheriff took the prisoners back to their cells. The Indians headed west toward their tepee homes.

Martha felt hungry, tired, and eager to see Willie and Rebecca. "Come on, Abe."

Willie hugged both Martha and Abe and couldn't quit talking. Rebecca, now three months old, smiled big toothless smiles. "I think she missed us," Martha told Abe.

The next morning Martha and Abe got up earlier than their usual five o'clock to do the chores and to give away and sell the milk. Abe hadn't even gone to the barn yet when Josie announced intruders. Almost at once, several men arrived on horses, demanding to talk to Abe.

"Ya heard what happened in the night?" one of Abe's vigilance committee brothers asked. "I'll tell you what happened. A bunch of thugs broke into the jail, beat up the marshall, and took off with them vermin what robbed your Injun friends."

Martha couldn't believe her ears. "You mean the men on trial are gone? Escaped?"

The big bearded man nodded. "That's right. That ain't such good news fer your Indian friends, neither."

Abe sprang to life. "I gotta milk the cows and feed the cattle," he said. "Go round up whoever you can find. Let's catch those cutthroats and make 'em wish they'd stayed in jail."

The men roared approval and took off, pushing their horses hard.

Martha helped the men milk, strained it, set aside the many gallons she would give away, and poured the rest into cans to be delivered down town.

"What about the Indians?" she asked while Abe loaded the big cans onto the wagon. "They need to know."

"I plan to go by their places soon's I get rid of the milk," Abe said. "I'll be back after that."

Martha tried to keep her mind on the two children, while preparing for the washing and baking, but it wasn't easy. She took Rebecca and Willie and hurried across the creek to tell Cleve and Mandy. "I'll be ready to go as soon as I get my own chores done," Cleve said. "Don't let 'em go without me."

Martha went home and looked at the clock. Six minutes after six. Seemed it should be about noon, so much had happened already.

The men returned before Abe. Cleve rode across the creek and joined them. Martha couldn't count them but she thought there must be more than a hundred men and horses. The loud talk made Martha realize how unhappy the community felt at the early morning jail break.

When Abe finally came, Martha hurried to him, hoping for a moment alone with him. "How did the Indians take the news?" she asked in a hushed voice.

He grinned. "Silently. Like everything else. But you can believe they'll be on their toes."

The men rode off in a big cloud of dust, nickering horses, and masculine voices yelling and laughing.

Martha returned to the house to bake bread, scrub clothes, and wait. Six hours later she had baked the bread and fastened the clothes on the line, but she still waited. Strapping Rebecca onto her back, she helped Willie saddle the horses, and they went for a long ride, keeping their eyes wide open.

Back home again, Martha prepared supper. Surely Abe would soon be home, hopefully with the criminals all captured.

But it was not to be. Abe returned two hours later, after Martha and Willie had struggled to milk all the cows while keeping Rebecca happy. Abe said they hadn't caught sight of the men.

"Like they dropped into a crack in the ground," Abe said. "We checked every crevice in a twenty-five mile radius." A smile pushed the disappointment temporarily from his face. "At least the Indians don't have to be afraid. I stopped and told them."

Abe had had a hard day with no rest, no food, or water. Ebb had had only water from a dirty slough. "Know what kept me going?" he asked Martha.

Martha shook her head. "I'm not sure, Abe. Was it knowing you were saving the Indians?"

"No, Martha my own. It was knowing you were here waiting for me. We all got discouraged, but no one had you to come home to but me." He kissed her tenderly. "God gave me the greatest blessing, when He gave me you."

Martha felt all warm and bubbly inside. She had been waiting all day for Abe too. "I purely love you too, Abram my love. Thank You, God, for making us for each other."

❧

Life slowly slipped back into its usual grind. The vegetable gardens came up with vigor and so did the weeds. Martha strapped Rebecca to her back and worked as much as she could.

The next week *The Washington Statesman* said the jury had found the defendants guilty. "They must have known, to stage that dangerous jail break," Abe said, sipping coffee as they read the paper Friday evening.

One evening Adam Jensen, the attorney, stopped by. After they visited awhile about the jail break and other things, he looked at Rebecca in Abe's arms. "You heard anything from the baby's mother or father?" he asked.

Abe pursed his lips as he shook his head. "Not a word. We've done a little looking too. We really don't know whether they're both gone back East or if one or both are still in town. We're keepin' our eyes open, though."

The lawyer got up. "Well, I must go. Keep in touch. If you're still after adopting, we might be able to push it through one of these days."

"What did he mean?" Martha asked after Jensen left. "Is one of these days sooner or later than six months?"

Abe handed Rebecca to her and pulled them both into his arms. "I don't know," he said, "but if I was a bettin' man I'd bet it's less than six months."

⁂

One day Martha realized she couldn't keep Rebecca on her back all the time anymore. The baby wanted to play. She also wanted to be able to see Martha.

"Abe," she asked one evening after supper, "you're so good with your hands, I wonder if you could make me a cart for Rebecca."

"What do you have in mind?" he asked.

"Well, could you get someone to make you some wheels, something like wagon wheels, only smaller and lighter? You could make a cart for Rebecca to ride in. Maybe one I could push."

"Maybe Nate Butler could make us some wheels."

A week later Abe brought home two lightweight wheels

smaller than those on a wagon. He used light lumber and built a little chair with sides on it as well as a back. He fastened the seat on a little frame over the wheels, put a strap across the front of the chair to keep Rebecca from falling out. "There! Get that girl!" Abe said proudly.

Martha put a blanket into the cart first, then gently put the baby in. Abe fastened the strap around her so she couldn't fall out. Martha pushed the cart back and forth a little ways. "It's good, Abe. I think this'll work a lot better now that she's older. I'll try it tomorrow while I work in the vegetable gardens."

The next morning, before Martha had a chance to go outside to hoe weeds, Gray Wolf, Pony Boy, and Camas walked into her house. "Food," they all said.

Martha knew them so well by now, she could have told them she didn't have time. But she felt glad to see them and welcomed a chance to visit with them a bit. "You men just sit down and I'll make you some sandwiches," she said, knowing they understand most of what she said. Slicing some meat she had roasted last night, she made three huge sandwiches, put them on plates, and pushed them in front of the Indians. She asked God to bless the food and also each Indian. Then she put a tall glass of milk in front of each.

She sat down across the table from them while they ate. "I guess you haven't had any trouble with those bad men," she said, knowing the men were far away.

Gray Wolf swallowed a big bite. "Indians know where bad men. Cows too."

sixteen

Looking up from the harness he worked on, Abe saw the three Indians and Martha approaching from the back yard. Martha usually didn't interrupt his work unless it was important. Curious, he laid down the leather strap and went to meet them.

"Hello," he called.

"Good morning, Abe," Gray Wolf said, enunciating carefully.

"Hurry, Abe," Martha called. "These men have something important to tell you."

Abe shook each Indian's hand, giving them the respect they deserved. "What is it, friends?"

"Let's go back to the house so we can sit down," Martha said.

When they all sat in the main room, Abe met Gray Wolf's eyes. "I gather something's happened. Is everyone all right?"

Gray Wolf leaned forward, his face almost excited. Now Abe knew something had happened. Gray Wolf hardly ever showed expression, seldom even smiled. "Indians know men take gold. Know cows. Mountains."

Abe took in a big gulp of air. "Did you see the men who took our gold?"

All three black heads jerked up and down. "See in mountains," Pony Boy said.

"Cows too," Camas finished.

"What cows?" Abe asked.

162

Gray Wolf looked patient. "Cows men take."

Abe couldn't sit still. He jumped to his feet. "You mean the cows rustled here this year?" Three black heads nodded.

"Who are the men? How many are there?"

Camas held up seven fingers. "Men took gold. Three more."

"Where are they?"

Through much talking, and with Martha's help, the Indians made them understand the men were holding lots of cattle in a box canyon, a valley with mountains on three sides. The men had built a fence on the fourth side to keep the cattle in the canyon.

The Indians offered to lead Abe to the place. "Tryin' to capture that many men in a spot like that'd be way too dangerous," Abe said. "They'd shoot us like ducks on a pond."

The Indians shook their heads. "Drink much firewater," Gray Wolf said. "Sleep long sleep. Cows make much sound. Not hear Indians."

"How do you know all this?" Abe asked.

"Indians watch. Not shoot Indians. Not see Indians. Not shoot Abe. Not see Abe."

Abe looked at Martha whose laughing gray eyes indicated she thought the whole thing hilarious. "Tell me how this is funny," he asked, truly curious.

She burst out laughing. "Oh, Abe, it purely is. Here we've been fretting about where those men went while the Indians have been watching them. You can tell they've been watching a lot too."

"How many times you men been in there?" Abe asked.

Gray Wolf looked at his sons. They all shrugged. "Much times," Gray Wolf said. "Not see Gray Wolf. Drink firewater—sleep."

"Well," Abe said, "I don't know how to proceed but the men have to be captured. I think we'll have to share this with the vigilance committee." He turned to the Indians. "Is it all right if I talk to white men about this? When we get a bunch of men together we'll get you to help us."

Gray Wolf got to his feet. His sons followed. "Gray Wolf help catch bad men. Soon?"

Abe grasped each hand again as the men left. "Real soon," he assured them. He held up one, then two fingers. "In one or two days."

Gray Wolf nodded. "Indians go first. See drink firewater. See sleep."

Abe called the group together in his yard that night and told him what the Indians had said. At first the men thought it would be a suicide mission, but when Abe explained the Indians had been there many times at night and the men were always in a drunken stupor, they wanted to go that night. Abe told them they would have to take the Indians with them and that the Indians would scout ahead.

They decided to make the raid the next night. Besides the Indians, they would take fourteen men, seven pairs. Each pair would approach and apprehend one of the drunken men.

"Better take a few extra—in case those savages counted wrong," someone called.

"They aren't savages," Abe said. "And they count as well as you. But it's still a good idea. Anyone could make a mistake in a place like that. Or friends might drop in that night. We'll take three more pairs."

ð

The next night about nine o'clock Abe kissed Martha goodbye. "I'll be praying for you every single minute," she promised.

Abe told her he would be praying too. Then he mounted Ebb and headed southeast with the group of men. The three

Indians rode with Abe.

After riding two hours, they began climbing into the mountains. After another hour the Indians told the men to wait there.

Abe took advantage of the time to pray. "You know what we're doin' here," he said. "Thanks for carin' about us, God, and please go with us tonight so there won't be any bloodshed. Thanks, Lord."

You're welcome, Abe. Go, without fear.

Abe felt a tremendous relief. "Thanks, Lord. I'll bet You knew I was terrified, didn't You? Of course You did."

Over an hour later, Gray Wolf returned alone. "Men sleep," he said. "Come."

"How many are there?" Abe whispered into the dark.

"Men take gold. Three more."

They rode the horses another mile, then Gray Wolf insisted they leave them. Almost immediately Abe noticed a fence on his right. A large gate lay wide open. When the men all passed the gate, Gray Wolf closed it. As they moved into the canyon, Abe heard cattle lowing. The sound grew louder as they progressed.

After another half mile they reached a campsite with burning lanterns hanging in the trees. The barely-glowing coals from a campfire told Abe the men had been sleeping awhile. Then he saw the men. Some half sat on logs, hunched over with their heads on their knees. Others lay on the ground, seeming to be sound asleep, an eerie sight in the light of the flickering lantern light.

Abe signaled the men to come in. Each team chose a man and they all reached the men at once. The extra men served as scouts watching for anyone else who might be around.

Abe and his partner gently took their man's hands, put

them together behind him, and tied them securely. The man stirred but didn't awaken. Then they tied his feet tightly and attached the rope to the one holding the man's hands. "Now he won't do any kickin'," Abe whispered.

When they finished, Abe looked around. Everyone else finished soon. One man awakened, screaming and yelling as if he were being physically tortured. Abe heard the vigilante tell him to shut up but the man kept yelling.

"A little unnerving," Abe's partner said. "Seems he's yelling to someone to come help him."

Abe smiled in the dark. "Yeah. These other guys who slept through the whole thing." Slowly it dawned on Abe that they had forgotten one thing. How were they going to haul seven drunken men more than a mile to the horses?

Eventually the vigilantes went after the horses and tied the rustlers over the horses behind the saddles. *Should have brought extra horses,* Abe thought. Well, they'd take it real easy.

Before they reached Walla Walla, several of the men had awakened and yelled loudly the rest of the way.

"What we gonna do with these vermin?" someone asked.

"That there tree's still standin' south o' town," several answered.

"Let's take them to the jail," Abe said. "And finish what was started last week. Seems only right. I think we got them all but let's take turns guardin' the jail anyway."

When they reached the jail, Abe ran inside to see if anyone was on guard. He found one man sound asleep. "Wake up!" he yelled. "We got a whole jail full of varmints for you."

After a lot of confusion, all the men stood behind bars. Several men took their positions to guard. "We don't need none of you around here," the jail guard said. "You can see those cages're tighter'n a new shoe."

"Yeah, that's what we heard last week," someone said. "We'll just help out a little, while these boys're in there."

The next day the men were still caged, awake, and screaming obscenities at anyone who came near. Abe didn't hang around long.

A large group of men on horses went to the canyon and herded the cattle back, disappointed to find only about 150 head.

Abe went back to the jail. The men had yelled themselves hoarse, so the place seemed quiet. "Where's the rest of the cattle?" Abe asked one of the men who had beaten Camas. "There was near a thousand rustled last summer. That's not counting the ones the varmints already hanged took. Those cattle went back to the rightful owners."

The man spit at Abe. "Think I'd tell you if I knew? We never had no thousand."

Abe moved down to the other end of the cages, hoping the men there hadn't heard his discussion with the spitter. "How many cattle did you boys get?" Abe asked a man who looked to be in his late teens.

The boy looked frightened. "Ain't got no idea," he said quietly.

Abe thought a moment. "Been selling 'em off?" he asked.

The boy nodded. "Sellin' 'em to miners for meat."

Abe took a good look at the boy. "You look like a decent young man. How'd you get stuck with this bunch?"

The boy's eyes grew red as though he were about to cry. "I didn't have any money or food. No one would help me or give me a job. These men fed me, then made me help take cattle. I did it, knowing it wasn't right. My ma would cry in her grave if she knew what I did." He paused a moment.

"So would Pa."

Abe believed the boy. His grammar indicated he'd been raised in a genteel family, and so did his fine-featured face. "How old are you?" Abe asked.

"Tomorrow I'll be seventeen." The boy's entire body trembled. "If I live that long."

Abe reached through the bars and patted the boy. "You just rest and pray to God for help. You commit your life a hundred percent to Him and He'll figger out somethin'."

Abe talked to the other five, finding them hard, cruel men, not caring what they had done and seeming to care less what happened to them. Abe then asked the sheriff when the trial would be held.

"Why you need a trial?" the sheriff replied. "Ain't a one of 'em deny's takin' them cattle. I heard the vigilantes're out gettin' the tree ready."

Abe remembered the seventeen-year-old boy. "They may not deny doing it, but one is a young boy those other ruffians saved from starving, then forced into the gang."

The big man shrugged. "May be. Ain't none of my problem, er yours neither."

"But it is our problem. Would you want something like this to happen to your son? The boy's innocent, Buckley. That's what trials are for."

Abe wandered down the street to the office of Jensen, the attorney's. "Heard anything about a trial for the gang we brought in?" he asked Jensen.

Jensen shook his head. "I haven't been invited to participate anyway."

Abe told him about the boy and left.

❧

When Abe told Martha about the young boy, she demanded

they do something. "Will they take them and hang them today?" she cried. "We purely can't let them do that, Abe. Remember Melissa? She could have been punished for picking your pocket. And she was hungry just like that boy. I think God's telling us we have to do more to feed starving people, Abe."

Abe sat down at the table. "I agree. Something we gotta take up right soon. Let's go see what's happening."

Abe put Rebecca into her cart, fastened the strap, and yelled for Willie. Before they got out the door Jensen arrived. Martha poured coffee for the men.

"There's going to be some sort of a trial," the attorney said. "They asked me to defend the accused. Good thing you stopped by, Abe, or I'd have refused. I won't try to turn guilty men free, but I'll do my best for the boy. The thing'll be this afternoon at two o'clock. Thought you'd want to know."

❧

Abe and Martha arrived early enough to find seats this time. The hardened criminals didn't deny their guilt and didn't show any remorse or respect for anyone talking to them.

Jed, the seventeen-year-old, acted like a different kind of person. Abe could tell he impressed Jensen and also the judge. Jensen called Abe to the witness chair, giving Abe a chance to say he thought the boy would prove to be a blessing to the community if they released him. The jury returned a verdict after a fifteen minute discussion, finding all but Jed guilty. They ordered the guilty men to be "hanged by the neck until dead" that afternoon at sunset. They made Abe guardian of the boy, Jed.

Then Adam Jensen stood up. "I'd like to speak for most everyone here and thank our Indian brothers for locating these men and helping us apprehend them. Would Gray Wolf please come to the front so I can shake his hand?"

Martha gave the tall Indian a small shove. He walked straight and tall to the front of the court room. Jensen and Gray Wolf reached out together and shook hands heartily. "We're fortunate to have you men in our community," Jensen said. "Would you like to say something?"

Gray Wolf nodded. "Firewater bad." Many people laughed and audibly agreed. Someone started clapping and soon the whole crowd clapped and stomped their feet. The Indians marched out the door, straight, solemn, and tall.

Abe and Martha took Jed home with them.

Jensen arrived a little later. "I brought some adoption papers," he said. "If you still want to adopt that baby, I say let's do it now."

Martha gasped. "Would that mean no one could ever take her from us?"

Jensen nodded. "That's about it. And she's a mighty lucky baby too. I figure you folks are going to be a great asset to this town and the people in it for a long time."

They wasted no time getting the adoption taken care of. Now Rebecca Ann Noble was theirs for always—and William Robert Noble's little sister. Abe thought of Jed, also an orphan. Well, he wasn't going to even think of that at the moment.

That night as Abe started falling to sleep, God spoke to him. *You did well, Abe. You're My precious son. But you'd better build some rooms onto your house. Several of them. And don't forget the bathroom.*

A Letter To Our Readers

Dear Reader:

In order that we might better contribute to your reading enjoyment, we would appreciate your taking a few minutes to respond to the following questions. When completed, please return to the following:

Rebecca Germany, Managing Editor
Heartsong Presents
P.O. Box 719
Uhrichsville, Ohio 44683

1. Did you enjoy reading *A New Love*?
   ❑ Very much. I would like to see more books by this author!
   ❑ Moderately
   I would have enjoyed it more if _____

   _____

2. Are you a member of **Heartsong Presents**? ❑Yes ❑No
   If no, where did you purchase this book? _____

   _____

3. What influenced your decision to purchase this book? (Check those that apply.)

❑ Cover	❑ Back cover copy
❑ Title	❑ Friends
❑ Publicity	❑ Other_____

4. How would you rate, on a scale from 1 (poor) to 5 (superior), the cover design? _____

5. On a scale from 1 (poor) to 10 (superior), please rate the following elements.

___Heroine   ___Plot

___Hero   ___Inspirational theme

___Setting   ___Secondary characters

6. What settings would you like to see covered in **Heartsong Presents** books?_____

_____

_____

7. What are some inspirational themes you would like to see treated in future books?_____

_____

_____

8. Would you be interested in reading other **Heartsong Presents** titles?   ❑ Yes   ❑ No

9. Please check your age range:
   ❑ Under 18   ❑ 18-24   ❑ 25-34
   ❑ 35-45   ❑ 46-55   ❑ Over 55

10. How many hours per week do you read? _____

Name _____

Occupation _____

Address _____

City_____ State_____ Zip_____

VeraLee Wiggins

The Forerunners Series

__*Heartbreak Trail*—While Rachel Butler gains in strength physically traversing the legendary Oregon Trail, her heart struggles to keep pace and chose between to wonderful men. HP76 $2.95

__*Martha My Own*— Rescued more than once by the heroic and faithful Abram Noble, Martha and Abram resort to a marriage in name only so she can survive in Washington Terriory. HP83 $2.95

__*Abram My Love*—Abe Noble's love for Martha Lawford knows no bounds. Yet their tacit agreement—a marriage of convenience, one in name only—denies such feelings. HP92 $2.95

__*Misplaced Angel*—Rachel Dorland lives by this Scripture: In as much as ye have done it unto one of the least of these my brethren, ye have done it unto me. Soon Rachel finds herself so tired helping others that she can barely think. HP128 $2.95

__*A New Love*—Abram and Martha Noble wouldn't be where they are unless they trusted their Heavenly Father for everything. Together, in the fledgling Washington State, they have shared enough adventures for a lifetime, or so it seems. HP183 $2.95

··········Presents··········

Great Inspirational Romance at a Great Price!

Heartsong Presents books are inspirational romances in contemporary and historical settings, designed to give you an enjoyable, spirit-lifting reading experience. You can choose wonderfully written titles from some of today's best authors like Peggy Darty, Colleen L. Reece, Tracie J. Peterson, VeraLee Wiggins, and many others.

When ordering quantities less than twelve, above titles are $2.95 each.

Hearts♥ng Presents
Love Stories Are Rated G!

That's for godly, gratifying, and of course, great! If you love a thrilling love story, but don't appreciate the sordidness of some popular paperback romances, **Heartsong Presents** is for you. In fact, **Heartsong Presents** is the *only inspirational romance book club*, the only one featuring love stories where Christian faith is the primary ingredient in a marriage relationship.

Sign up today to receive your first set of four, never before published Christian romances. Send no money now; you will receive a bill with the first shipment. You may cancel at any time without obligation, and if you aren't completely satisfied with any selection, you may return the books for an immediate refund!

Imagine. . .four new romances every four weeks—two historical, two contemporary—with men and women like you who long to meet the one God has chosen as the love of their lives. . .all for the low price of $9.97 postpaid.

To join, simply complete the coupon below and mail to the address provided. **Heartsong Presents** romances are rated G for another reason: They'll arrive *Godspeed!*